Tobermory Tales

stories • from • an • island

Lorn Macintyre

Argyll
publishing

© Lorn Macintyre 2005

First published in 2005 by
Argyll Publishing
Glendaruel
Argyll PA22 3AE
Scotland
www.argyllpublishing.com

**FT
Pbk**

The author has asserted his moral rights.

British Library Cataloguing-in-Publication Data.
A catalogue record for this book is available from
the British Library.

ISBN 1 902831 78 X

Cover photo: stockscotland.com/John Macpherson

Origination: Cordfall Ltd, Glasgow

Printing: Mackays of Chatham Ltd

In fond memory of Chris Dillon
dear friend, Gaelic mentor

Acknowledgements

The Winning Way was published in *The Laughing Playmate:
Scottish Short Stories 1992* (HarperCollins)

The Man from the Sea was broadcast on BBC Radio 4

Contents

Foreword

Lorn Macintyre's first collection of stories, *Tobemory Days*, was published in 2003. It established the locale of their setting as the island of Mull. The book set the young impressionable eyes of the character of Marsaili – the girl growing up in a fading culture of Gaelic language and being – as the filter through which life passed. It placed the character of Archie Maclean, the Tobermory bank manager, as the conduit of the lives of Mull people, past and present. The book has been a critical and commercial success.

It is therefore a pleasure, as its publisher, to write a foreword by way of context-setting for this new book, *Tobermory Tales*. The author has made no secret of the fact that the character of Archie the bank manager is based more than loosely on his late father. Lorn Macintyre's family moved when he was a youth to the bank house in Tobermory when his father took up a position there.

Macintyre senior was delighted with the posting because it took him nearer his beloved Gaelic language. And in the days when a bank manager, like the minister and the teacher, was a pivotal figure in the community, it was as if all life passed through their house.

The young Lorn Macintyre attended school on the mainland in Oban and was clearly receptive to the narratives of life in all its detail. The rich result is available to readers of these books.

As the poet John Donne wrote in 1624, 'no man is an island, entire of itself', yet it is as if in these stories from an island, island status brings an accentuation of aspects of the lives of people. When the world around is changing fast, a rural island location and culture pose their own brand of question on the human condition. Who stays and who leaves? Who arrives from the outside and for what motive? What is contained within and what is freely expressed? Questions that might equally be asked of the individual as of the community.

And there is the shared history. The most overtly historical and political story in this book is Dispossessed. Which of the many generations of the MacKinnon family that were named Uisdean made a success of life, and which could be said to have failed? The Uisdean who, under threat of eviction, eloquently represented himself and his kind to the Napier Commission in 1883 on the future of crofting? The Uisdean who went to die young, like so many Highlanders, in the Boer War? The Uisdean who just ran his croft, worked unloading the cargo boats and eked out a tolerable life? Or the Uisdean who is jailed for setting fire to a neighbour's holiday home built on the former MacKinnon homestead out of sheer frustration and grief?

Like the great story writer, Alice Munro, whose material comes from another perhaps unpromising, and to the eye of the unperceptive visitor, fairly dull, rural setting of south-western Ontario, Lorn Macintyre's stories are a joy because they are layered in meaning. Five years in jail for malicious fire-raising can be banal; it is often the endgame of a sequence that encapsulates the human condition.

There are numerous themes that can be identified in this rich tapestry. A hunger for new ideas or a discontent with a feeling of marginality can lead to personal compromise and embarrassment in The Winning Way; it can also end in near catastrophe in Living on Love. An over-earnest cherishing of native culture and placing past history as a burden on the shoulders of the young is exposed with all their unintended consequences in The Cradle of Life.

And it is the conflict of the generations in the face of fast-paced change that points up the ambivalences of island life. It does so in urban life too, but the conflicts are more dissipated. As in the baldly written Ecstasy, the young of a small and socially limited community can yearn for the anonymity of the city, where the appeal of mass media holds a promise of becoming the person you might be. If only.

Readers of *Tobermory Days* and this new book *Tobermory Tales* who are looking for a romantic or sanitised view of life in the Scottish Highlands and islands will be disappointed. You should look elsewhere. Some of the themes are dark, but no darker than life can be, and just as light and joyful as it sometimes is. Just as his late father Angus was a fine relater of narrative in the oral tradition, Lorn Macintyre is a very good writer of stories that entertain and stay with you sometimes into the wee small hours and for days afterwards.

It gives me particular pleasure as a publisher operating in the same Argyll locality as the setting of the action in these books to bring this material to a national and international readership. Enjoy.

Derek Rodger
Argyll Publishing
April 2005

1
Undeliverable

Another yellow package has come off the steamer, brought hot-foot up to the bank house by Marsaili. That evening she helps her father to set up the projector in the sitting-room, lifting the lithograph of the stag at bay from the wall and closing the curtains against the seductive light. Alice takes her place in the front row as her husband breaks open the package and threads the slim film through the sprockets of the projector.

Archie Maclean is an erratic film-maker. His favoured position is the small tower off the sitting-room, where he likes to stand, filming the worthies as they come along Main Street, past the clock and the tempting window of Black's with its array of whiskies. One of the most telling scenes in the large collection of home movies in the box with the corroded catches under his bed shows Tormod MacTavish with his carry-out.

It was a frosty afternoon near the festive season, with the Christmas tree already lit at the clock, and as Tormod slipped in his hob-nailed boots the carry-out broke on the pavement. From his tower eyrie the banker filmed the distraught Tormod going down on his knees beside the amber pool, looking as if he wanted to lap it up like a thirsty dog, until he was helped to his feet by two sympathisers and walked between them across to the Arms where a few drams restored his belief in living.

This evening Archie is showing a film he had shot a fortnight before while out walking with his wife at the top of the town. As the substantial residence at the end of the lane comes into view, it looks as if the island is being struck by an earthquake, the way the landscape and the building are tilting. Yet it is possible to make out a small man emerging from the creeper-covered porch of this villa. He wears khaki shorts and a blue cap with a tassel, several sizes too small, on the back of his head.

'Who on earth is that?' Marsaili enquires.

'That is Dr MacNaughton,' her father informs her from behind the whirring projector.

Dr MacNaughton is seen descending the three broad steps to his front lawn. He stretches in the fine evening, then begins to touch his toes, laying his palms flat on the turf among the daisies. Then he lies on his back and begins to pedal his short stocky legs in the air.

'He's off his head,' Alice pronounces from her privileged seat.

'I've never seen him before,' Marsaili says, laughing at his antics.

'That is probably the most peculiar person on an island that has many peculiar people,' the banker pronounces. 'He's an ogam expert.'

'Ogam?' Marsaili queried.

'The series of marks which the Picts are supposed to have used as a writing system. Our friend here doing his exercises on the wall apparently decided that he wanted to revive ogam, so he started addressing his letters in it.'

'Was he doctor here?' Marsaili asked.

'By the grace of God, no. He went to Edinburgh University to study medicine in 1921 and graduated in 1942. He then went abroad to practise, in Africa, they say, so it's impossible to calculate by how much he reduced the native population in his short career out there. I'll tell you this, though, I certainly wouldn't let him near me, even if I were at death's door. In fact, I would go further: I would prefer the professional services of Dr Murdoch, and we all know his record with the living and the dead.'

'What's that he's got on his head?' Alice wanted to know.

'His shinty blue cap from Edinburgh University. He's so proud of it, like a little boy. There is an example, Marsaili, of love of Gaelic carried to fanaticism by a learner. I dread when he comes into the office. If there's time I hide in the safe when I hear his voice, otherwise I'm subjected to half an hour's tirade in Gaelic, full of words that nobody uses nowadays. Besides, his accent's terrible.'

Having done his callisthenics on his lawn, Dr MacNaughton went indoors for dinner. The spacious villa, really a small mansion house, had been built in 1875 by his father who was descended from an old island family who had made a fortune droving cattle, swimming them across the sound to the mainland, then down to the Falkirk Tryst. From sleeping in their plaids beside their herds, and waking with frost on their faces, they had acquired a fine house with feather beds, bathrooms, and generous fireplaces.

When Dr MacNaughton returned from his sojourn in Africa, he gave up medicine in favour of Celtic studies. His grandfather had been a native Gaelic speaker, but after his marriage to a member of a prominent Edinburgh family, his wife had forbidden him to pass the crude language on to their children, since, she insisted, English was the language of civilised discourse.

The entrance to the MacNaughton villa is through a conservatory, with a venerable vine that has wandered over the granite wall for nearly a century and still provides grapes for the table, because this island, despite the heavy rain, is washed by the Gulf Stream.

Thirty years ago Dr MacNaughton had a noted classical scholar to stay, and after dinner they adjourned to the conservatory with their malt whiskies, to watch the sun sinking into the ocean. Dr MacNaughton's father, who had had a classical education at an English public school, had taken a pot of gold paint and printed an inscription in Latin round the wall, above the productive vine. The translation read something like: 'It is pleasing to sit on the great land and watch those working on the great sea.'

'What does that quotation mean?' Dr MacNaughton asked, putting his distinguished visitor to the test.

The classics prizeman from the Edinburgh Academy studied the gold lettering in the fading light.

'It means: fuck you, I'm all right, Jack.'

On the left, along the corridor, lined with nineteenth century prints of Highland chieftains, some of them foxed, is the drawing-room, a clutter of pictures and furniture, because Dr MacNaughton has a weakness for the mystical figures favoured by Hornel, particularly children who look like spirit beings playing in shrubbery.

Next door is Dr MacNaughton's library, which was the morning-room in his parents' time. Their son had the walls lined with quality bookcases that came on the steamer, and which had once adorned the library of a notable country house in the south that had had to be demolished through dry-rot.

These transplanted shelves hold one of the largest libraries of Scottish Gaelic and Irish books in private hands, because, since he developed his obsession with Gaelic at the age of eighteen, Dr MacNaughton has had dealers in Scotland and Ireland and even further afield searching for volumes on the lists he has provided them with. There, third shelf along, is a copy of the Jacobite poet Alexander MacDonald's Gaelic Dictionary, signed by the author. There are only three surviving copies of Thomson's Gaelic guide to the Flora and Fauna of the Hebrides, and one of these, albeit with new binding, is on the second shelf fourth along.

Dr MacNaughton is now shifting the ladder hanging on rails

from his shelves. He moves it along and his stout legs ascend the rungs to the top. He brings down a folio under his arm and carries it to his standing desk, opening it as if he is about to deliver a sermon. This is a book on ogam script. Much of it is conjectural, taken from the rubbings of ancient stones, but Dr MacNaughton is convinced that he can reconstruct the ogam language from it, a project he has been working on assiduously since his return from Africa, where natives scratching communications with sticks in the dust gave him the idea. Many a night Mrs MacNaughton, up in her draughty bedroom on the first floor, has heard the squeak of the ladder, followed by her husband's cry of contentment at having recovered another ogam mark.

Ten years ago Dr MacNaughton began to address his letters in ogam, and when they came back stamped 'undeliverable; unknown language,' he wrote to the Secretary of State for Scotland, pointing out in a five thousand word essay that ogam was one of the languages of Scotland. The Secretary of State wrote a polite reply, pointing out that even if the ogam language were still in use, 'it is extremely doubtful if we could recruit letter sorters and postmen who could decipher it.'

But this rebuff hasn't deterred Dr MacNaughton from continuing with his ogam studies. Not tonight, however. He switches off the light and goes upstairs to his bedroom, and through it to the dressing-room. He likes to keep the mirror on the table at an angle of thirty eight degrees, for a reason he has never shared with his family. Every morning when the maid dusts the mirror she moves it, and every evening, after having restored its angle with a large protractor, he writes with chalk on the glass (in English, not ogam): '36.7 degrees. Try again.'

Every three months a barrel is slung ashore from the cargo boat and hoisted up on to a lorry which conveys it up the hill to Dr MacNaughton's residence. This is his regular order of Guinness, direct from the brewery in Dublin, and as he removes the bung he fills the frothing jug. Some years he has black bantam hens, and other years white ones, in the wire-netting enclosure behind the house, where he gathers the eggs in a basket.

On the day of the Grand National Dr MacNaughton pulls down all the blinds in the house and goes about with a black armband, because fifty years before an uncle broke his neck at Beecher's Brook on an outsider.

There are those in the town who say that Dr MacNaughton is a genius. Others maintain that it would be a kindness to lead him by the hand on to the steamer for conveyance to the nearest mental institution on the mainland. The banker is in the majority of those who are convinced that Dr MacNaughton is 'not all there.' Gille Ruadh, who helps his mother and sister to run the local telephone exchange, and who is in the bank house six nights a week, drinking whisky and divulging information he has gleaned from eaves-dropping on phone conversations, is blunter than his host. Dr MacNaughton is 'deranged'.

On this particular night Archie has left his projector set up, so that Gille Ruadh can view this rare sighting of the ogam expert, filmed in action on his own lawn.

Sipping his generous dram, Gille Ruadh watches the scholar's callisthenics with a mixture of contempt and pity.

'He's a bloody nuisance,' the visitor avers, in one of his rare uses of improper language in front of his venerated hostess. 'He comes on the phone, asking for a number in Gaelic, but I can't make out what he's saying. When I ask him to repeat it in English he answers me in Gaelic. My mother was on the switchboard one night and he started talking to her in Gaelic and she lost her temper and shouted at him in Gaelic: "get off the line, you bloody fool!" but he didn't understand what she was saying and went on talking, so she just pulled the plug on him. The worst thing is, he's convenor of the dancing at the Games, and we can't get rid of him. He goes up to the competitors and tells them that they're doing the Highland Fling wrong because he has an old book in his library which shows it being done in a different way. Then he gets up on the platform to show them and leaps about as if he's got a wasp in his shorts.'

'His wife must have a hell of a time with him,' Alice observed.

Gille Ruadh turned to his attractive hostess, offering her a Gold Flake from the pristine packet.

'She bears her burden in silence.'

The following summer Marsaili saw the ogam expert in the flesh up on the Games Field. He was in charge of the dancing competition which she was taking part in and in which she had high expectations of the trophy. He was wearing his khaki shorts and blue cap with the gold tassel. As she came out of the changing tent he was kneeling on the platform, applying resin so that the dancers wouldn't slip, though there hadn't been a drop of rain for days. The Sword Dance was called and he emerged from his lean-to with a pair of claymores.

'My ancestors fought with these against the MacNeils of Colonsay,' he informed one of the judges. 'The MacNeils came here in their galleys, but we were waiting for them, and we cut off their thumbs so that they couldn't row home again. One of my relatives collected three bucketfuls of thumbs from the shore.'

He took so long to get the crossed swords on the platform exactly right, measuring the angle of intersection with a protractor, Marsaili's leg muscles were getting stiff, waiting to dance. Her father, who was wearing the Treasurer's rosette in the lapel of his tweed jacket, came over and asked Dr MacNaughton politely to get the competition going. That provoked ten minutes of discourse in Gaelic neither Marsaili nor her father could follow.

While all this was going on a junior race was being started with a pistol. The boy who breasted the tape with his arms out kept running, and then he was rolling on the ground. The banker ran towards him, thinking he was having a fit, but he had swallowed a bee on his way to victory. It had stung him in the throat, and he was getting blue in the face. His mother was standing wailing as he writhed at her shoes. Dr Murdoch wasn't on the Games field that day, because he had a rendezvous with fairies down the island, so the Treasurer ran across to the loudspeaker to ask if there were a doctor among the crowd.

Marsaili saw Dr MacNaughton running across the park and pulling a *sgian dhu* from the hose of a piper as he passed.

'Carry him in there,' he instructed the boy's bearers, pointing to the tent.

Oh God, Marsaili thought, remembering what her father had said about the ogam expert's medical record in vulnerable Africa. *He's going to operate on the boy.*

But he didn't go into the tent with the lethal blade. Instead he seemed to be staring at a spectator sitting on the hillside, enjoying her picnic. Dr MacNaughton scrambled up the slope, snatched the sandwich from the woman and as he came down he threw away the chicken filling. Marsaili could see into the tent as Dr MacNaughton forced the bread into the boy's mouth and made him swallow it. It took the sting with it, and immediately the doctor used Bushmills whisky from the little flask in the pocket of his shorts to reduce the swelling in the boy's throat.

That evening Gille Ruadh visited the bank house to discuss how the Games had gone. The weather had held, and there had been record takings at the gate, with several long-standing records broken. But these weren't the main topics of conversation between the Secretary and the Treasurer.

'Dr MacNaughton saved that boy's life,' the banker conceded.

'He certainly did,' Gille Ruadh concurred, finishing his substantial dram before going across to take the money at the door of the Games dance. 'Evidently it's an old remedy he read about in a Gaelic book. The mother was so grateful that she's going to donate a cup for the Highland Fling.'

It would be good to report that Dr MacNaughton lived to ninety, and that eventually he persuaded the Secretary of State for Scotland to accept his ogam script, and to send postmen to night school to decipher it.

Dr MacNaughton died at the age of eighty two, peacefully, in his khaki shorts, his shinty blue cap on the back of his head, in his wicker chair in his conservatory above the sea, the gilt letters from the classical quotation still readable after seventy years.

2
Home Boy

On the way across the moor he stopped on the cliffs, to look down on the sea breaking on the rocks far below, the next landfall America. For another mile the heather whispered round his shins before he saw the tumbledown farmhouse, the outbuildings nailed together from flotsam. He had to hammer on the door for a good minute before an old woman came shuffling.

'If it's drinking water there's a burn over there,' she told him, her smell sour.

'I'm collecting Gaelic stories and I heard you were a great tradition-bearer,' he said to her in Gaelic.

'Who told you that?' she asked suspiciously, her shoulder seeming to support the askew lintel.

'The School of Scottish Studies in Edinburgh.'

'You're an American, aren't you?'

'No, I'm from Nova Scotia.'

'I had an aunt out there. She'll be long since dead.'

'Had she family?' he enquired.

'Three children.'

'Maybe I can look them up,' he offered.

'In that case you better come in.'

He followed her into the primitive kitchen with its flagstoned floor and black grate in which timber from the sea was sparking. He noticed the paraffin lamp on the dresser as she cuffed the hostile cat from the sagging seat for him.

'I understand you're the last person in the area with Gaelic,' he began.

'My husband had it, but he died years ago.'

'Do you live here alone?' he enquired.

'They wanted to put me into a home in the town, but I told them I was going to die here. I came here seventy years ago as a girl of eighteen.'

'Don't you have any help on the farm?' he continued.

'We used to have two men, but they died. I keep a few sheep, that's all.'

'I'm told you have a lot of Gaelic stories,' he said, reaching down to unzip the Canadian Pacific holdall between his trainers.

'What's that you've got there?' she asked sharply.

'A tape recorder. I'd like to record a few of your stories.'

'I don't want my voice put on that,' she said with fear as well as anger. 'Anyway, I don't have the electricity.'

'It's battery operated,' he informed her. 'You have such beautiful Gaelic, it would be a tragedy if it wasn't preserved, especially when you're the last speaker of this particular dialect of the island.'

'I don't care about it being preserved. It did me for most of my life, until I lost my husband and didn't have anyone else to speak it with. What will you do with the recording?'

'I'll play it to my students in Nova Scotia, so they can hear how Gaelic should be spoken.'

That seemed to please her, and he was allowed to run the recorder.

'What's the first Gaelic story you heard?' he prompted.

'I got a lot of them at my mother's knee. We never spoke any English in our family. In fact, you could go for months without hearing a word of English spoken in the district, until the tourists came in the summer.'

'You didn't welcome strangers?'

'They didn't understand our ways.'

She began to tell him a Gaelic story about a young man who appeared on the headland one day.

'No one knew how he'd got here. It was thought that the fairies had brought him across from the west, because he had such beautiful Gaelic. He got work on one of the farms, doing the hardest jobs, such as ploughing a field full of stones. The people laughed behind his back and said, 'he'll never do it,' but he did, stopping the plough and lifting away huge stones as if he had supernatural strength.

'Every task they set him, which they thought was impossible, he completed. They sent him out one night to fish for mackerel, knowing he wouldn't get any off the cliffs, because it was too dangerous with the tides. But when he rowed back at dusk they were up to his knees in the boat, beautiful fish that the people salted for the winter.

'And then, one day, someone came from Ireland, and it was found that he was a prince of the blood royal who had been sent out here to prove himself.'

'Did he punish the people for what they had done to him?' her visitor asked.

'I don't know the end of that story. But I'll tell you about the creature that was a seal by day and a woman by night. She came out of the sea to seduce men and left them mad, searching for her on the shore.'

After three hours all his spools of tape were full.

'Were your folks from here?' she enquired.

'Why do you ask?'

'Because of your Gaelic. It's as good as my own,' she complimented him.

'No, they weren't from these parts. From further south. What kind of help did you have on the place in the old days?' he asked.

'We had a couple of dummies. They were good workers, but they died.' She tapped her white head. 'Folks who don't have it up here don't live long.'

'Did you have anyone else helping you?' he continued.

'No, that was all.'

'Was there a boy here once?'

'Who told you that?' she asked, watching him.

'Someone I was recording in the town mentioned a home boy who was here once. They said that he disappeared.'

'Disappeared?'

'He went over the cliff.'

As he was pushed down the gangway of the steamer the suitcase he was carrying with someone else's initials in the corner burst open and his only other shirt and underpants were scattered over the pier. The woman coming off behind him cuffed his head as he scrabbled to put his few possessions back into the case. In her tight grey uniform, her hair in a bun, she looked like one of these women who had been recruited as Nazi camp guards. All she was lacking was the German Shepherd dog by her side.

The awkward boy was pushed on to the bus which took him northwards along a single track road on which they didn't meet another vehicle for miles.

When they got off there was a walk along a bleak headland. He needed the toilet, but there was no cover.

'Hurry up, I have to get back on the afternoon bus,' the woman warned him as he wiped himself on the abrasive heather.

The house at the end of the headland was grey, surrounded by outbuildings which had been constructed from flotsam, including a stateroom door from a torpedoed liner.

'So this is the home boy,' the woman who answered the door said contemptuously.

She was thin in face as well as body, in a faded floral apron.

'What's this one's name?'

'Alasdair MacNally.'

'I hope he's a good worker,' the woman said.

'He had a job in the school holidays in a bakery,' his attendant stated. 'We got quite a good report on him. A bit clumsy, but willing.'

She took the attendant into the kitchen where she signed the papers, as though she were buying a calf.

'Send me a report every month,' the attendant requested.

'I'll do that all right. If he's no good you can come and take him away again.'

As the attendant was disappearing into the distance the woman was leading the boy outside, behind the house.

'You see that?' she said, pointing to a heap. 'That's to be lifted on to the cart there. Use this,' she instructed, pulling the pitch-fork from the earth and thrusting it at him.

When she had gone back inside he stood looking at the stinking heap of manure until she rapped on the window. But every time he tried to use the fork the manure slipped through the prongs and flopped on his boots.

'This is the way you do it, you fool!' she shouted, snatching the fork from him and sinking it into the heap. She lifted the manure and tossed it on to the cart. 'If you can't get the hang of a simple task then you're no use to us.'

An hour later the heap had been transferred to the cart and he was leaning on the fork. The tears in his eyes weren't from exhaustion or the stench: he was wondering what he had done to deserve this. He had known nothing but a succession of institutions since his mother had put him up for adoption in the city. In the first one he had been bullied by the other inmates, who were illegitimate like himself, and who took out their anger and hopelessness on him.

When they told him that he was being sent 'up north' he had borrowed an atlas from the school library and lain on his bed, something you could be punished for doing during the day. The north coast was far away from Glasgow with its noisy streets and its blows to his body and head, and he began to imagine he was going to a place where a maternal woman would boil him eggs fresh from under the hen, and hear his prayers before he went to sleep, with a window open on a calm sea.

This place on the headland was even worse than the home in Glasgow, the woman harder on him than the housekeeper who put too much salt in their porridge.

It was getting dark, and all the dung was up on the cart when the woman rapped the window and signalled him in. There was a man sitting at the end of the table, a spoon in his fist, and two other men on either side. The woman said something in a strange language and the man at the head of the table glanced at the boy as he raised the brimming spoon to his mouth.

The woman pushed him towards the chair, and he sat at the bowl of soup. The two men on either side of him who were wearing their caps back to front on their heads put their fingers into the corners of their mouths and pulled faces at him.

When the boy reached out for a piece of bread she struck his fingers with a knife.

'You'll ask if you want something in this house. You're not in Glasgow now, with the rest of the trash.'

The three men got meat, but there was nothing more for him except a cup of tea. He was too frightened to reach for the sugar bowl.

'You've got an early start in the morning,' the woman warned him. 'Show him where he's sleeping,' she ordered the dummies.

They led him across the yard to a flight of steps going up the side of the building. The room at the top had coombed ceilings, and two mattresses lying on bare boards.

One of them pointed to another stained mattress lying in a corner.

The only place to put his clothes was a chair with a broken

back that had come out of the sea. He turned his back to undress, the two dummies sniggering behind him. When he turned one of them was waving his penis at him.

The bed in the home in Glasgow had been hard, but at least it had been his space, with a narrow wardrobe and a drawer. He lay down on the stained mattress, closing his eyes to say his prayers, asking to be returned to the city as soon as possible.

The two dummies were communicating with their fingers in the way that the boy had seen the Three Stooges doing on a rare visit to the cinema in Glasgow. As he tried to sleep a rat ran across his legs, and one of the dummies threw a wellington boot at it.

The boy felt a hand under the blanket. He struck it away, but one dummy pinned him down while the other one did to him what the other boys had used to do to themselves in their audible beds in the Glasgow dormitory. He was shouting but no one came up the stairs.

Next morning the mattress was kicked from under him by the woman.

'It's gone six,' she warned him.

He put on the same clothes he had arrived in and went down to the kitchen where his breakfast was half a bowl of thin porridge and a cup of tea, whereas the three men got a fry.

'Time to get that dung spread,' the man said in English, taking his cap from the back of the chair.

The boy stood on the trailer as the grey tractor jolted across the field by the sea. His job was to spread out the dung with the fork, but the tractor was going too fast.

'You're making an awful arse of it,' the man complained, braking. He came round and jumped on the cart. 'What do they teach you in the city?' He showed him how to hold the fork, flinging the manure away from him.

As the light was beginning to fade over the sea he had got into the rhythm of it, but he was exhausted, and on the way home on the empty cart he was falling asleep. Supper was tough mutton.

The woman and the man talked in Gaelic, sometimes turning to the dummies to rebuke them for their table manners. The boy knew that he was being isolated, but he also knew that he wouldn't be left alone when he went up to the loft, so he was grateful when the woman gave him another task, sawing up lengths of timber salvaged from the shore. It was dark when he stacked the last pieces of firewood against the wall of the house, and when he groped his way up the stairs he saw that the dummies were lying on their mattresses.

But as soon as he lay down they were across at his mattress, one of them pinning his arms by his side while the other interfered with him. When he saw it was hopeless struggling he closed his eyes and imagined that he was walking in sunlight along sands somewhere, his mother waiting for him with a picnic, a cloth spread with cakes and lemonade, the treats that they only got at Christmas in the home in Glasgow.

They worked him from morning till night, and fed him less than the others. When it came Saturday the dummies were given a half crown each to spend at the mobile shop that came to the end of the road, but he only got a shilling, the coin tossed across the table to him by the woman.

After the man had cut the glistening black bank of peat, assisted by the dummies, the boy was sent by himself to carry the blocks of fuel in a creel on his back a mile across the moor, and when he didn't stack it properly, the way the woman had shown him, she lashed out with a knotted rope.

One evening he didn't come when the woman called supper.

'I'll give that little bastard such a hammering,' she told the dummies as they pulled faces with their fingers in the corners of their mouths.

When the boy didn't come the man went out to search for him. Two hours later, he put a pair of boots on the kitchen table.

'Where did you find these?' she asked.

'On the cliff. He's gone and drowned himself.'

'He was no use here anyway,' she said. 'That kind never are.'

'They'll come asking questions,' her husband warned her.

'Let them come. Who's going to tell them anything?' she challenged him. 'Not these two anyway,' she said, nodding towards the dummies.

The old woman turned her head and looked out of the filthy window towards the sea.

'There was a boy here, a long time ago. He drowned himself.'

'Why?' her visitor from Nova Scotia persisted.

'How would I know? You'd better be going, now you've got what you came for.'

'No I haven't,' he said. 'I want to show you something.'

He unzipped the Canadian Pacific bag and handed her a book.

'I bought this years ago,' he told her. 'It was my first Gaelic book. It cost five shillings.'

She put on her spectacles to read the underlined phrases.

'I saved up the shilling you gave me to go to the van with, and I sent for the book. I went to meet the postman every day until it came, because you would have taken it off me.'

'You can't be the home boy,' she said, shutting the book.

He put his fingers into the corners of his mouth and pulled.

'I thought, they're speaking Gaelic because they want to exclude me, but I'm going to learn the language so that I know what they're saying about me. I couldn't study the teach-yourself Gaelic book at night because the two dummies interfered with me, but I took it out and memorised the words as I was working. And I listened to you speaking Gaelic with your husband so that I could get the pronunciation.'

'The home boy drowned himself,' she said.

He had left his boots on the cliff so that they would think he had thrown himself into the sea in his unhappiness. Then he had hobbled across the headland in the too tight wellingtons that belonged to one of the dummies. A fish lorry had given him a lift to

Glasgow, where he had laboured at the docks, studying at night, so that he could get the qualifications to take a degree in Gaelic. Then he had gone out to do a doctorate at St Francis Xavier University in Nova Scotia.

'You've stolen my Gaelic,' the old woman was shouting, hauling at the bag on his shoulder. 'Give me these tapes!'

'You stole part of my life, and I've stolen your Gaelic, so now we're quits,' he told her as he went towards the door. 'I'll publish these tales in a book of traditional stories I'm putting together, and it'll help me to get a chair of Celtic in Scotland. And when I'm letting my students hear your story about the boy who came from Ireland and turned out to be a prince, you'll be dying out here, beyond the cliff, in loneliness and squalor, with no one to care for you, no one to speak Gaelic with.'

3
Mortal Remains

In the attic room of the Hebridean Hotel a young woman from another island was keeping vigil, fingering the little Celtic silverwork cross between her breasts as she watched the dark sound beyond the bay, her lips moving in a silent Gaelic prayer. The steamer from the mainland was late because of the heavy sea running in the sound, and her lover was in the engine room. She could see him bending over the juddering pistons, wiping his brow with an oily rag, trying to keep steam up against the ferocious Atlantic.

A crowd was huddled together on the pier, some of the wives of the crew wailing because they were sure that the steamer with their menfolk was at the bottom of the sound. Suddenly the love-smitten girl in the hotel attic saw the unsteady mast light appearing above the island at the entrance to the bay, like a wavering star coming to earth. She clattered downstairs and out through the sun-lounge, on to the terrace. The wind was forcing her back but she clung to the balustrade, leaning over and yelling to those on the pier below: 'It's coming! It's coming!'

As the steamer approached the pier a coiled rope came out of the darkness and was caught by one of the stevedores who secured it to a larger rope, dragging the noose to the bollard. Down below, the whey-faced galley boy was sweeping up the china shattered in the crossing. When the gangway was hoisted into position the passengers staggered off. Most of them had been violently sick for the duration of the voyage, and one elderly man, a retired Colonel, lay with a suspected heart attack in the purser's bunk.

Everyone was turning away for home, arms linked with their loved ones when a figure appeared on the deck. Someone shouted and pointed, and everyone turned into the force of the wind to stare. The man at the top of the gangway was carrying a coffin on his shoulder. This was not the normal way for a body to travel home for burial on the island. The coffin would be shouldered aboard by the crew at the mainland port, then laid on the floor of a small saloon below, with the feet pointing west, to *Tìr nan Òg*, destination of the dead. On calm days a Bible would be placed on the nameplate, to give comfort to the occupant on his or her last voyage up the sound. On stormy crossings the sad cargo would be roped to the brass rings in the floor of the saloon.

But this coffin hadn't been down in the saloon. It had lain on the floor in the corner of the bar where the stranger who had brought it ashore on his shoulder was sitting drinking large whiskies, with no concern for the waves crashing against the portholes and the shuddering of the steamer, as if at any moment the fifty year old rivets were going to spring at the unbearable pressure of the sea. When the steamer lurched again he put out a boot to steady the coffin.

'What a way to treat someone's remains,' an old woman sipping a cherry brandy to settle her stomach lamented in Gaelic.

A farmer who had been to the mainland to get an infected tooth pulled came up, cap in hand, to try to read the name on the coffin, but the man travelling with it leaned across and covered the brass plate with his palm. Then he started to whistle a pipe march, keeping time with the toe of his boot on the coffin. When it slid away from him again he yanked it back by one of the brass handles.

By the time the steamer entered the comparative shelter of the bay he was well away with drink, draining his seventh double before hoisting the coffin on to his shoulder. As he went up the stairs to the gangway the other passengers stood back out of respect, and one of the few Catholics on the island crossed herself. At the top, as he lurched past the purser's office, the stranger's burden struck the wall and almost slid from his shoulder.

There he stands, at the top of the gangway, the coffin on its side on his shoulder, the crowd on the pier watching him in horrified apprehension as he comes unsteadily down the gangway. At the next step they expect the coffin to slide from his shoulder and smash open on the pier, revealing its contents.

Then one of the stevedores standing in streaming black oilskins shouts in Gaelic: 'In the name of God, it's Cailean Macdonald!'

They lived in one of the crofts at the top of the town and were among the poorest of the poor in a community that knew what poverty was because of the enduring effects of the potato famine in the mid nineteenth century, when the starving had crowded into the town, to find that the meal sacks for the destitute were long since empty.

The five Macdonalds relied on two acres of boggy ground, two cows and the odd jobs that Seumas Macdonald could get – when he was fit enough to work. He died from tuberculosis at the age of thirty two, coughing his bloody lungs into the basin his wife held out to him in the hovel. The parish had to bury him in a coffin as basic as a potato box.

The three children went barefoot to school, and while the other pupils ate their sandwiches the Macdonalds gnawed at raw potatoes. There was talk of the family being taken into the Poorhouse, but Mrs Macdonald was determined that her children would not be subjected to that final indignity, so she rose at six, to peel a sack of potatoes in the scullery of the Hebridean Hotel, went home at eight to see her children out to school with porridge in their bellies, then at ten o' clock went to clean the manse and other properties in the town.

She pleaded with Munro the joiner until he took the oldest boy Cailean on as an apprentice, pointing out that he was good with his hands, and one Christmas had made for her a beautifully carved panel on the Nativity scene which she venerated as though it were a priceless icon.

Cailean was a quiet, attentive boy who watched Munro carefully, and soon learned to use the range of planes and the different types of saws. Within two years he was fitting windows in the impressive villa being built at the top of the town by Sandy Forsyth, who had made a fortune in haberdashery in Glasgow.

One night Peigi Macfarlane up at the top of the town asked Cailean to repair the bottom of her door, which a rat from the nearby burn had gnawed. Cailean did the job perfectly and was given five shillings, which he gave to his mother. But Peigi was known for her big mouth and told the folks in the shops what a wonderful job the apprentice had made of her door. 'And so cheap too.'

When Munro heard about it he turned on Cailean.

'You've no right to be doing jobs on the side. Give me the five shillings.'

'I gave them to my mother,' his apprentice told him truthfully.

'Then you're sacked.'

In the annals of a town such as this, the truth sometimes becomes distorted. It was said that Cailean left on the morning steamer to get work on the mainland, while others insisted that he had waited a week. At any rate, he ended up in Glasgow.

As Cailean Macdonald shoulders his way into the Arms with the coffin on his shoulder there are horrified gasps from the customers standing at the counter.

'You can't bring that in here,' Carmichael warns him.

'Why not?' Cailean challenges him.

He is very drunk and Carmichael doesn't want any more trouble, having nearly lost his licence for causing a mutiny on a visiting minesweeper after selling hooch to its crew. The coffin is slid from Cailean's shoulder and pulled by its handles to the fire, as if the occupant can benefit from the warmth. Cailean asks for and is served a large whisky, and takes his glass to the fire to sit beside the coffin. The men at the counter are uneasy and watch him in the gilt mirror advertising whisky above the crowded gantry of bottles they will help to empty. Cailean's mother is long since dead, but the drinkers are trying to remember if any of the two brothers, or the sisters, had gone to the mainland, because one of them is probably the occupant of the coffin. But one brother emigrated to Australia, where he prospered, and the other is up in the cemetery beside his parents. Beathag, one sister, is married to a shepherd at the other end of the island. Her death has certainly not been reported by word of mouth; not has it been in the local paper. Catriona, the other sister, is a matron in an Edinburgh hospital. Is it she who is in the coffin at her brother's boots by the fire in the Arms?

Since they have never bothered with Cailean's family in the past – and certainly never helped the mother when she was widowed and left with the five children – they daren't express condolences about his sister, who had a fast reputation when she was a student nurse. Instead they buy Cailean drams, and soon the table is cluttered with glasses. He shouts '*Slàinte!*' as he raises each one, toasting his benefactor before draining it.

At ten o' clock he gets to his feet. As he hoists the coffin on to his shoulder it begins to sway and two men go forward to steady it and ask him if he needs help, but he declines politely. As they hold open the door for him they assume that he is going up to the church with his burden. They will report this incident to their spouses when they go home, and it will enter the folklore of the town.

When Cailean first arrived in Glasgow as a seventeen year old it was the hungry thirties and he found it impossible to get work, though he trudged round dozens of carpenters' shops. He had no money and he slept under bridges in the bitter weather, pawning for bread and cheese the few tools he had managed to buy on his poor wages from Munro. On the seventh day he wandered down to the river, thinking seriously of ending it all in his despair, but as it was still a Christian world in those days a man in a bowler hat in a shipyard took pity on the thin youth with his soles showing through his boots.

He loved being on the high scaffolding, working on the transatlantic liner with the carpenters, helping to lay the pine decks. His work was so neat that they let him into the staterooms, where the walnut he was planing was worth more than a month's wages if he made a mistake. As he fitted the vanity unit he imagined a woman in an evening gown, like the laird's lady at home, doing up her face in the mirror as the liner sped across the Atlantic.

He had lodgings in Partick, residing with a woman from Lewis who spoke only Gaelic with him, and who served him heaped plates of potatoes and salt herring to build up his strength, leaving him with a raging thirst. But at that time he had never been in a pub. He sent ten shillings a week home to his mother and wrote neat affectionate letters to his brothers and sisters, telling them that he was learning to dance at the Highlanders' Institute, but finding the schottische difficult. He went to church every Sunday morning and was generous with his donations to the plate the islander with the rheumy eyes proffered, along with thanks in Gaelic.

Cailean began to court a pretty dark-haired nurse from the Western Infirmary who hailed from the island of Bernerary and who told him that her ambition was to have four children and live in one of the new council houses in Knightswood. Her name was Eilidh and one night he kissed her in the dark doorway of the mortuary room in the Infirmary.

He was present when the liner he had helped to build was

launched by a titled lady who swung a bottle of champagne against the graceful bow. The liner had a bustle of chains to slow its progress into the narrow river. Next day, the foreman told Cailean regretfully that the yard didn't have another order, and that therefore he was out of work. He wrote him a glowing reference and advised him to become a Mason.

Cailean wandered the streets of the city and was down to his last five shillings, and owing his landlady a fortnight's rent. She told him that she could keep him for another week, and if he hadn't paid employment by then, she would have to rent his room to someone else.

Going to bed in her cottage that night, the devout Ealasaid McCormick saw the glimmer of a light in the Macdonalds' abandoned croft house, and asked herself why the dead should come back to such a place when the Bible guaranteed rest after the labour of life.

Next afternoon Baxter the policeman parked his car on the verge and walked across the muddy pasture to the Macdonald croft, where he found the door open, and Cailean sitting drinking a cracked mug of tea at the table, his stockinged feet up on the coffin.

'It's against the law to keep a dead body,' he cautioned Cailean, taking his notebook from his pocket. 'Where is the death certificate?'

'I lost it.'

'You lost it?' he said incredulously as he wrote.

'I lost it on the boat last night.'

'Whose name was it in?'

'That I can't remember.'

'You're making a fool of me, Macdonald.'

Three days after being laid off from the shipyard, Cailean saw a notice in the evening paper he retrieved from a bin.

WANTED: SKILLED CARPENTER

FOR HIGH-CLASS CITY UNDERTAKERS

He put on his Sunday suit and went along to be interviewed by the managing director.

'What was your last job?'

'Fitting out the staterooms in the *Empress of Caledonia*. And beautiful they were too, of walnut. One mistake and that was a month's wages forfeited.'

Next morning he was making his first coffin, for a leading city lawyer. The widow with a fox fur at her throat and perhaps too much lipstick for a mourner ordered that no expense was to be spared: the finest mahogany, heavy brass handles with red tassels, an engraved brass plate. The Archbishop and a dozen priests would be on the altar at St Aloysius for the requiem mass, with interment thereafter in the family layer at St Conval's. The managing director praised his new carpenter's handiwork, and when the widow came in to pay the account she slipped him ten shillings.

Over the years Cailean was to make many coffins, of all sizes, in many different types of wood. But it wasn't like fitting out a stateroom. The quality boards he had so carefully planed and screwed together were reduced to ashes along with the contents in the crematorium, or had a ton of earth shovelled on their polished perfection.

It was the Glasgow Fair, and because of the good weather and the opportunity to get down the water to the coastal resorts, not so many people were dying. On his third slack afternoon Cailean was at a loss for work. He had already tidied up the woodstore and sharpened his tools. Then he had an idea. He lay down on the workshop floor, making a chalk mark behind his head on the boards, then stretched beyond his boots to make another mark. Then he got up and went into the woodstore.

'I don't recollect ordering this coffin,' the managing director said when he saw the work of art in African mahogany standing in its gleaming magnificence on trestles in the middle of the workshop.

'It's for myself, sir.'

'Stop fooling, Macdonald.'

'It's true, sir. I made it for myself.'

'You made a coffin for yourself out of our best wood and brass?' he shouted, banging a handle as he walked round his carpenter's handiwork. 'I was keeping this mahogany in case the Lord Provost or another civic dignitary passed away.' ('Died' was a word not used in this high-class undertakers.)

Cailean was sacked on the spot, and that night he broke into the workshop and stole his own coffin. He decided to go home to the island, and for the first time in his life he tasted strong drink in his disillusionment on the stormy voyage down the sound. When he sobered up he did up the family croft house, lining the walls with tongue-and-groove boarding. He also laid a new cement floor and put in a stove.

The coffin was kept under his bed. He had put it on castors and when anyone called he pulled it out to use as a table, with the result that the African mahogany became stained with the rings of tea mugs, and scorched where cigarettes had been balanced on the edge to free the mouths of visitors for the recounting of a tale in Gaelic.

Cailean Macdonald died of a heart attack while planting potatoes on his croft.

4
Living on Love

Jessie McCabe was the first female postwoman on the island.
Rory, the previous postman, had carried shrapnel from Montecass-
ino in his legs across the moors in all weathers until he was forced to
retire. Jessie got the job, and her daily round included a five mile
circuit of the moor on the southern part of the island. The Post
Office provided her with a cape, but she still got soaked on stormy
days when the ballast of the mailbag seemed to be the only thing
that was keeping her from being blown out into the ferocious sea.

The parcels in the bag weren't part of her delivery. The girl had
a good heart, and when Urquhart in the village shop asked her to
take a bag of sugar to an old woman who couldn't get to the shop
herself, how could she refuse?

Jessie, who was in her teens then and attractive, her long dark
hair held back from her face by one of the elastic bands from the
bundles of letters, developed strong calf muscles from her daily
hike. Add to this the fact that her mother had been a champion

Highland dancer, and that was why Jessie came away from the island games with cups clinking in her bag. Sometimes, on a calm morning on the moor, she would slide the heavy delivery from her shoulder and practise the Reel of Tulloch among the swirling butterflies, her hands raised above her head like a sprite.

Her elderly customers loved Jessie, not only because of her cheerfulness, but because she spoke Gaelic, and even if she had no letter for a house, she would stop for a chat, to please the occupant. To these isolated women and men this was better than receiving a letter, and they would bake scones especially for her, pushing more of them into her pockets before she took her leave with a Gaelic blessing. They would stand at the gate, watching her crossing the moor, her cape rising like red wings in the breeze.

There was one house where Jessie never stopped with letters or for a chat. It was a house by the shore, halfway through her delivery, and she would halt on the hill to look down on it. Jessie had enquired about the house on her rounds, and had been told that it had belonged to Donald, an old crofter who had lived alone, without electricity or running water.

'He was a queer one, all right,' the postwoman's informant revealed, her hand on the pot she intended to offer her visitor more tea from.

'In what way queer, Annie?' the postwoman prompted.

'Well, he never had a vet near his beasts in his life, and he lived till he was over eighty.'

'Was that because he was too mean, Annie?'

'No, no, he would give you his last penny, if he thought you had a need. He wouldn't use a vet because he didn't require to.'

Jessie smiled and sipped her second cup of tea. Talking was different from delivering mail, because this old woman had all the time in the world and stories, unlike letters, didn't date.

'Are you saying that he didn't need to use the vet because his beasts were so healthy, Annie?'

'They were healthy because he cured them himself.'

'And how did he do that, Annie?'

'I've seen him myself, as sure as I'm sitting in this chair, talking to you. This cow had bad colic, from eating something from a bog. Its stomach was twice its size, but he laid his hands on it, and I watched it going down, like a balloon that had been pricked. He got a reputation as a healer, and people used to bring their animals to him from miles away. I remember one old man who walked from the other end of the island to get Donald's help. Of course Sydie the vet wasn't pleased because he was from the mainland and was a greedy man, wanting the fees.'

'So why is there nobody in Donald's house?' the postwoman asked, before she went on her way.

'Oh it was a good house, there's no denying that, because when a boat was torpedoed during the war and its cargo of wood washed ashore, Donald used it to line the house and put a new roof on it. You've never seen a better job,' the old woman said, moving her hand along an imaginary wall of pine boards, perfectly tongued and grooved.

'So it's the factor who won't let anyone have the place?' the postwoman asked, reaching for her bag by the door.

'It's nothing to do with the factor. It's because they say that Donald's still there.'

'But you said that he was dead,' the postwoman said, hoisting the bag on to her shoulder at the open door.

'He died years ago, but they say he's still seen.'

'Have *you* seen him, Annie?'

'I haven't, but then I haven't been near the house in years, because my legs wouldn't carry me there. But I'll tell you this, lassie, seeing him again wouldn't frighten me, because he was a good man with a gift from God in his hands. If you had heard that poor cow bellowing that day, then going away with its tail swinging after he'd cured it of the colic, you'd know what I mean. Be sure to call in again tomorrow.'

But Jessie didn't call in the next day. Instead she did something that she had never done before: she went down the slope to Donald's cottage. The door was hanging open on one rusted hinge, and sheep had used the place as a shelter, their droppings littering the flagstoned floor. Jessie ran her hand over the pine boards, the gift from the sea that Donald had fitted to the walls, but they were discoloured by the weather that had entered through the broken windows. It was hard to imagine that this had once been a cosy home.

The next time she called on Annie, Jessie reported the state of the animal healer's cottage.

'They would be as well knocking it down,' the old woman said. 'It's sad, seeing a place like that going to rack and ruin. But of course people want their home comforts nowadays, though I've never missed the electric. My paraffin lamps will see me out.'

Then, one morning, Jessie saw smoke coming from Donald's house and surmised that tinkers were squatting in it. They came to the Ross in the summer to collect whelks, which they sent away in small sacks on the steamer to mainland markets and because they were industrious, could earn quite a lot of money for the season. Not that Jessie had ever carried a letter to a tinker because, of course, they had no fixed abode, and she had heard her father say that they wouldn't be registered for tax or national insurance. In other words, tinkers didn't exist officially. But they certainly were a presence on the island, pitching their bow tents on the same stances, year in, year out, always by a burn. In the old days they had dealt in horses on the island, using (her father told Jessie), a private form of Gaelic called Cant, so that strangers wouldn't know what they were discussing – which was usually how little they were willing to pay for a horse.

Many of the islanders were frightened of tinkers, convinced that they had the power to leave a curse at a house where they didn't get a can of tea and something to eat, which, Jessie's father said, only encouraged them. He claimed that they would steal anything as soon as your back was turned, and that they were better off than most folks on the island. He cited the case of a tinker who had been found dead by the roadside, with hundreds of pounds on him, but couldn't remember where this had happened on the island.

So Jessie wouldn't be going down the slope to converse with the tinkers who had obviously occupied Donald's house. But the woman who emerged didn't look like a tinker. Jessie slung her bag from her shoulder, and sitting on her heels, watched her. The woman had good features, even from that distance, and her clothes looked as if they had been made for her at one time. Jessie saw her crossing the rocks with unsure steps, then standing looking out to sea. She stood there for perhaps two minutes, then appeared to bow to the ocean before going inside.

Jessie was even more intrigued when a man appeared with a pail. He went down to the shore and, having set down the pail among the weed, began to gather what the watching postwoman took to be whelks. Now what was all this about?

But Jessie had an unusually big delivery that morning, and had to get on her way. She didn't even have time to stop in at Annie's, to give her the news that Donald's house was occupied again.

Two days later, as Jessie was sorting the letters in the post office, she came across a strange name and address.

'Where is this?' she asked the postmistress, who ran the shop and post office combined.

'It's old Donald's house, by the shore. A couple came in a week ago and said their mail was being sent to this address.'

'But Donald's house doesn't belong to them,' Jessie said indignantly.

'It belongs to the estate, but they don't seem to be interested in it. Good luck to them, though I can't for the life of me think why anyone would want to stay in that hovel.'

Jessie decided not to tell old Annie in case the thought of Donald's house being occupied by squatters upset her. However, two days later, there was a parcel to deliver to the house. Jessie hesitated on the slope, wondering if she could slip down and leave the delivery on the step without being noticed. But if the wind – it was a blustery day – blew the parcel away, then she would get the blame.

She knocked the door and the woman opened it, looking even younger than she had done from the top of the slope.

'Thank you,' the stranger said, holding the parcel against her breasts, as if she already knew that the contents were precious. 'I would offer you a cup of tea, but we don't have any.'

Years later, when Jessie re-ran this conversation in her head, she would ask herself, why did I say:

'I could have brought you some from the shop'?

'It's not that we forgot to buy tea,' the woman told Jessie. 'We can't afford it.'

The postwoman was confused and didn't know what to say. She was turning away when the stranger touched her arm.

'Even if we can't offer you proper hospitality, do come in.'

Jessie could have made the excuse that she had a heavy delivery that morning, but it wasn't true and besides, her curiosity had got the better of her, so she slung her bag from her shoulder. The interior was cleaner than when she had looked in a few weeks before. The sheep droppings had been scrubbed from the flag-stones, and cardboard had been taped against the broken panes. The man she had seen on the shore with the pail was sitting on an upturned lobster box salvaged from the sea, reading a book.

'I am Sheila, and this is Paul,' the woman made the introductions.

Jessie introduced herself as a bench was pulled out from the table for her.

'You're the postwoman?' Sheila said. 'It must be very hard, going round in bad weather.'

'You get used to it,' Jessie told her. 'I'm surprised to find this house occupied.'

'This is what the Lord wanted,' the man said, closing his book.

Jessie wasn't sure that she had heard correctly, since the man had an English accent. By the Lord did he mean the Duke, who owned most of the Ross, including this house?

'I came here following a crisis in my life,' Sheila explained. 'I was living in the south, but one night a voice told me to come to this island. I didn't have the fare, but I set out on the road with my suitcase and got a lift on a lorry. I didn't have money for the ferry, but the Lord always provides, and when I was standing on the pier a man came up and handed me a pound. Then I got a lift from the ferry to this place, and I started to walk along the shore with my case. I came across this house and knew that this was where I needed to be, so instead of going back to the mainland I stayed here, and last week Paul joined me.'

'We met on a train in Devon five years ago,' Sheila explained to Jessie.

'Sheila was reading a book,' Paul came in to the conversation. 'It was about the spiritual life and we began to talk about that subject. We discovered that we had both been searching for something beyond our ordinary lives.'

It began to sound like a rehearsed double act to Jessie as the woman took up the story again.

'I was teaching the violin in London. I had conscientious pupils, and was making a comfortable living, but there was something missing in my life.'

It was Paul's turn again. 'I ran my own successful business, but I wasn't fulfilled either. I had read so many books, searching for a way forward, and then I met Sheila on the train.'

'I had heard the voice years before,' Sheila recalled. 'During the war I worked in an underground bunker, with a huge map on a table. We went round it, using a long wooden rake like a croupier to pull off our planes that had been lost. I remember one night during the Battle of Britain, we almost had to clear the map.

'I was going home one dawn after a particularly heavy air raid.

Streets were just heaps of rubble around me, really, with firemen hosing them down and bodies being carried away. I had never felt so depressed. I said to myself: this war is going to end in defeat. I am going to be killed, or I will end up a slave of the Nazis. That's when I heard a voice saying: "no, you will survive, to do my bidding." '

Jessie was embarrassed by this revelation, and didn't know what question to ask next. When she was ten an itinerant preacher had come off the steamer, a tall, stern looking man carrying a black bag, with his white starched collar cutting into his Adam's apple. That night he had held a prayer meeting in the hall, and the corrugated iron building seemed to shake as he thumped his fist on the table on the stage, shouting: 'You are all sinners who need to be brought to God!'

The first person to rise to his feet and go forward was a mentally retarded man who worked on a farm, and who wore his cap backwards. He made faces and shouted out as he passed their house, but Jessie's parents had assured her that he was harmless.

Now he was coming forward, with his pronounced ears and silly giggle, his cap pressed to his chest. When he reached the platform he stood looking round in bewilderment, as if he had forgotten why he had come out, then went down on his knees in front of the platform.

'Is there only one sinner among you?' the preacher on the platform demanded, smiting the table again with his fist.

Others rose from their seats in various parts of the hall, and soon there were about twenty kneeling in front of the platform. The preacher began to berate them for being sinners, and they became so upset that they cried and called out that they would never be saved. In front, with his cap pressed against his strong heart, the mental defective looked around him and beamed.

Jessie's parents hadn't gone down on their knees that night. On the way home her father had explained that he had seen an even bigger conversion as a boy, when almost the entire village had gone down on their knees in the same hall when a missionary had disembarked from a sailing boat, a massive Bible under his arm as he was carried ashore on the back of one of the boatmen.

'The biggest drunkards on the Ross were suddenly devout teetotallers,' Jessie's father recalled. 'They joined the Band of Hope and walked about with armbands, stopping to ask people if they had signed the pledge. Some of the converts lasted a couple of days, then went on massive benders. I remember that Calum Ruadh broke his wife's arm and had to be taken to the mainland handcuffed between two constables, the brute.'

'What happened to the loony?' Jessie asked.

'He kept on laughing till the end, and when he died at the age of eighty, up at MacCall's farm, he had his cap on back to front in bed. He was wiser than the ones who had been converted. He was daft, but not daft enough not to see through the preacher. He went out to the front of the hall to get the attention, you see, because everyone ignored him when they passed him.'

As she stood listening to the couple in Donald's croft Jessie was beginning to suspect that they had come to convert the island. They were wasting their time. The old didn't need converting, and the young wouldn't go to church, because they stayed up so late listening to Radio Luxembourg through aerials they had rigged up specially. There was even talk that part of the village store was going to be converted into a café, with a jukebox ordered from the mainland.

Jessie decided to warn these two well-meaning people that the island was barren ground for them.

'But we're not here to convert anyone,' Sheila said. 'That isn't part of God's plan.'

Jessie would have liked to hear what God's plan was, but she was already late with her delivery. They urged her to call again, but as she went up the slope she was glad to get away from them. She hadn't intended to call on Annie, but there was a rare letter for her, and the postwoman gave an account of the two squatters in Donald's former abode.

'They've no right to be there,' the old woman said vehemently.

'They seem to think they have,' Jessie said. But she hadn't the time to explain about the voice the good-looking female had heard among the fires and smashed buildings of wartime London. Besides, this information would only upset Annie further, and, if she took a stroke, could lie for hours helpless in her house.

The two squatters disturbed Jessie. Were they menacing? She didn't think so. Deluded? Very likely. They were certainly intriguing. As her father would say in his expressive Gaelic, there was a story there. It wasn't necessarily the story the woman had told her about hearing the voice of God in the Blitz.

She wasn't sure if she believed Sheila's story. If she had a mission from God, then why this island? Why not Glasgow with its gangs? Wasn't the word of God needed more in the crowded city than on this island, with its miles of desolate moors, its bracken-shrouded ruins? The two evangelists were a century too late: the emigrant ships had long since departed for the new world.

There had to be another explanation for the presences of the man and woman, too poor, apparently, to afford a packet of tea. Certainly their clothes had looked shabby, and she had noticed that one of the sandshoes Sheila had been wearing was worn through at the toe. But had there been a Bible in that room? This was a question Jessie carried into her sleep, and she dreamed that night that her bed had been transported to that reclaimed house by the sea.

The next morning Jessie delivered a packet of tea, biscuits, and a pint of milk, paid for out of her own pocket.

'We knew you were coming with these gifts; that's why we have the kettle on,' Sheila told the postwoman.

'How did you know?'

'God told me early this morning. You must stay for a cup of tea.'

Jessie's bag, which she lowered on to the flagstones, was light that morning. She sat round the table that Donald had made from the leftover timber. Sheila put a cracked cup in front of her guest.

'Tell us about yourself,' Sheila urged.

'There isn't much to tell. I deliver the post once a day. That takes up until two o' clock, and then the next day's post comes in at four o' clock on the boat, and I sort it for the morning.'

'But you like your work?' Paul prompted.

'I like the landscape, and meeting people. The only sad part of it is when a letter brings bad news. One morning I left a letter at a certain house (she didn't name the occupant) and I was only a hundred yards away when I heard her wail. Her brother had been killed on a whaling ship in South Georgia.'

'So you went back to comfort her ?' Sheila asked.

'How did you know?'

'I know the type of person you are. What are your interests?'

'I'm a Highland dancer.'

'Really?' Sheila said, leaning across the table.

'Then you're blessed,' Paul told her. 'Dancing is part of the spiritual life. Gurdjieff knew that.'

Jessie asked for the name to be repeated.

'Gurdjieff was a mystic. He had an Institute for the Harmonious Development of Man at Fontainebleau in France. Dancing was an essential part of the activities. I know this because I met a woman in London who had lived at the Institute for five years. She was a wealthy society woman, very cultured, but her job there was to look after the pigs.'

Jessie's expression showed that she wanted to hear more about this intriguing place.

'Gurdjieff taught dances that, he said, he had learned from Dervishes. You must dance for us sometime.'

'What do you do for food?' Jessie asked the question that had been occupying her all the way across the moor.

'We gather whelks,' Paul said.

'But you can't live on whelks,' the postwoman protested.

'They're nourishing,' he said simply.

Jessie didn't want to offend them by telling them that whelks were the food of the tinkers. They obviously couldn't afford meat. By the looks of them they couldn't afford anything. They were thin, and Jessie wondered if these were their only clothes. What were they going to do when the winter set in, when there were days when the wind drove her backwards with her mailbag, days when you would be drowned by the waves in attempting to gather whelks?

'One can live on love,' Sheila said.

Jessie didn't know what to make of this. Were these two married, or living together?

'We can live on the love of Christ,' Sheila elaborated. 'It's a matter of raising one's vibrations.'

Jessie was lost, but didn't want to show her ignorance.

'If we do everything unto the Lord then our vibrations are raised. Even through gathering whelks.'

'We do that too with love, because a whelk is part of God's creation,' Paul came in. 'It is nourishment supplied by God with love, and this raises our vibrations, our spiritual energy.'

Jessie wanted to ask seriously if the tea she had brought could do the same, but she was finding that she was having to concentrate very hard in order to try to understand what these two were saying. Because, even if it were nonsense, they obviously believed it most earnestly. In fact, Jessie had come to the conclusion that Sheila had a lot of love in her face, the way she looked at you.

'How can I raise my vibrations?' Jessie asked.

'Oh you must do that already through your Highland dancing,' Paul told her. 'You move with grace and joy because Christ is there, with you. Think of it this way. When a young ballerina is being trained, very often there's an adult dancer behind her, holding her by the waist, helping her to master the steps. When you do the Sword Dance, Christ is behind you, stopping you from stepping on the blades. In the same way he is behind us on the shore when we are gathering whelks, his arms round our waists, stopping us from falling into the sea.'

'And what about when I'm out on delivery? Is Christ with me?'

Jessie wanted to know.

'He's with you, helping you with the heavy weight of your bag, making sure that you don't fall.'

Jessie wanted to ask this question: how could Christ accompany every postman and woman on earth on their rounds – assuming that there was only one Christ? But she was already confused, and was also late.

'Christ sent you with this tea for us,' Sheila said. 'We thank you for it, and we will thank him later in our prayers.'

This morning, though Jessie had a letter for old Annie, she decided to hold it over until the next day. She wanted peace and quiet to think about what the two had said to her, so when her bag was lighter she stopped on the moor, closed her eyes and tried to feel the vibrations that Sheila had spoken about, but all she experienced was the breeze from the sea whipping her waterproof trousers against her shins.

Next morning, before she went to collect her mailbag, Jessie took four rashers of bacon and two eggs from her mother's fridge. She wrapped the food carefully in strips of newspapers and put it into the big pockets of her waterproof jacket.

There was no mail for Donald's house, but she delivered the bacon and eggs.

'This is too kind of you,' Sheila protested.

Jessie watched as Sheila broke the eggs into a blackened pan she had found in one of Donald's cupboards. She stood by the stove, watching the bacon blistering. Before the two of them ate from plates that had many dark veins running through them, they said a prayer. Jessie bowed her head.

'This place is so clean,' Jessie observed.

'Cleanliness and godliness are very close,' Sheila informed her. 'There's no point in doing a job, however menial, unless you do it to the best of your ability – and with a smile. When Paul and I first came to this house we spent hours on our knees, scrubbing the sheep droppings from the flagstones. There were times – usually late at night – when I felt like saying, this floor is clean enough, but I knew that Christ wanted us to go on, to make it as clean and perfect as we could, so that when we eventually collapsed into bed, it was with the knowledge that we couldn't have done any more. Would you want to invite Christ into a dirty house?'

Jessie wanted to laugh, but saw that Sheila was serious.

'There's a new age coming in which all these things will be explained,' Sheila predicted.

'When is it coming?' Jessie asked.

'It's almost upon us,' Paul elaborated. 'Our spiritual masters are working to give us their spiritual knowledge and healing powers.'

Jessie resumed her round, and this time delivered the letter to Annie. It was a catalogue for wool.

'The couple in Donald's house are very religious,' Jessie began.

'Are they Catholics?' the old Free Church stalwart asked with a frown.

'I don't know what they are. But they say that the most important presence in their lives is Christ.'

'It's the *curam*,' Annie diagnosed.

'What's that?'

'It's something people get on the islands of Lewis and Harris. A girl from Lewis worked beside me when I was in Glasgow. She smoked and took a whisky, and she went to dances in the Highlanders' Institute and sometimes allowed men to take her home. I was worried she would get into trouble, because she was a very good-looking young woman. Anyway, she went home for the summer holidays, and when she came back she was a changed person. She'd been out at a dance on Lewis, and was lying in bed when she said she saw a radiant light by the window, and knew that Christ was in the room with her. Evidently he told her that he was disappointed with her way of living in Glasgow.

'When she came back to Glasgow she was a changed person. She wouldn't go near the Highlanders' Institute, and wouldn't touch a drop of drink. And if you swore in front of her she would leave the room, shaking her head. I shared a room with her and every night she was down on her knees by her bed, praying.

'It was the *curam* she got when she went home to Lewis, you see. That's what can happen to them up there. They can be converted in a night, and stay like that for the rest of their lives. My husband used to say, thank God there's two things we don't have on this island – foxes and the *curam*.'

'But the two people in Donald's house aren't from Lewis,' Jessie pointed out.

'But they could have gone there for a holiday. I suppose it's harmless, so long as they keep it to themselves. Years ago a man came to this door, saying he was from the Jehovah's Witnesses and would I like to buy their magazine. I told him he could turn and go back the way he had come, which was miles across the moor. I would keep away from these two if I were you, dear. Just push their mail under the door.'

But Jessie went down the slope each morning, though she didn't have letters to deliver. Her mailbag contained food she had stolen from her mother's kitchen – half a loaf, a pot of home-made jam, two slices of luncheon meat. Sheila and Paul always said a prayer over the gifts before they devoured them in front of their bearer.

'Why don't you come and see us this evening?' Sheila invited Jessie.

On the way back from her round Jessie went into Urquhart's shop and bought a chicken which she put into her mailbag. But she didn't put it in the kitchen for her mother. Instead, she hid it under the bed, along with the carrier bag of potatoes she had taken from the sack in the shed. She would have taken one of her father's lettuces too, but knew that he would have missed it, because he was growing them for the local produce show.

Jessie put on her jacket and slipped out of the house with her bag while her parents were listening to the Gaelic news on the radio. As she walked across the moor she wondered if this was a wise thing to do. She seemed to be getting very friendly with the two strangers, and kept thinking about what Sheila had said about 'raising one's vibrations.' In fact, she had sat very quietly in her bedroom for two successive nights, trying to feel these vibrations, but nothing had happened. Perhaps the two squatters in Donald's house were cranks. Should she be wasting her hard-earned money taking them a chicken, and the potatoes her father had planted on their croft?

'You shouldn't have brought this,' Sheila said as she unwrapped the chicken.

She banked up the stove with driftwood before putting the chicken into the oven, and Paul washed the potatoes at the sink. Sheila suggested that they go for a walk along the shore while the supper was cooking.

'What did you mean about a new age coming?' Jessie enquired as they walked by the calm sea.

'A new age of spirituality. But it isn't going to be expressed through formal religions, because that's too limited. Nor is it going to be organised, with a programme. I am to help people to see God in their lives.'

'And I am her disciple,' Paul said as he walked on the other side of Jessie.

'Paul has been called upon to make many sacrifices for me,' Sheila revealed.

'What do you mean?' Jessie asked.

'I left my wife and family to follow Sheila.'

Jessie stopped in shock.

'I had an electrical goods business in Brighton,' Paul went on, taking her arm and moving her forward. 'We had a fine house on the seafront, and holidays abroad as a family. I have two sons.'

'You left them?' Jessie asked.

'After I met Sheila on the train I realised that I had to follow her. I explained it all to my wife, but she isn't a spiritual person.

The parting was very acrimonious, but it had to be done. I gave her the business and the house, so the three of them aren't short of money.'

'I knew we would meet,' Sheila said when they were back in the warmth of the house.

'How did you know?' Jessie queried.

'I knew it long before I saw you.'

'Have you the second sight?' Jessie asked in wonder.

'The second sight?' Sheila asked.

'It's when someone sees what's going to happen. My grand-mother had it. She could tell when a person was going to die.'

'Only the Lord has that power,' Sheila said sharply, a tone Jessie hadn't heard her use before.

'But you said that you knew we would meet,' Jessie reminded her.

'That's different from knowing that someone is going to die. I got a message from the Lord about you.'

'A message?' Jessie asked, bewildered.

'God sends Sheila messages,' Paul revealed. 'It's been going on for a year now. It happens every night. Sheila is instructed to write down messages.'

'The message last night was about you,' Sheila told the postwoman. She read from the notebook she took from a shelf. 'Jessie is to join your mission. She is the third of you, the triangle.'

'What does it mean, joining your mission?' Jessie asked apprehensively.

'It means making a total commitment to Christ. I'm not talking about going to church and saying your prayers. That's easy to do. I'm talking about living your entire life through Christ.'

How was Jessie supposed to fit this in with being a postwoman?

'Will you dance for us?' Sheila requested as the potatoes were knocking against the lid of the pot on the stove, and the kitchen was filled with the aroma of roasting chicken.

'I need music to dance to.'

'No you don't. The music should be inside your head,' Sheila told her. 'Dance for Christ, Jessie.'

Jessie decided to do the Reel of Tulloch, her fingers almost touching the low ceiling as she wove round the table to the sound of bagpipes in her head.

'You're a beautiful dancer,' Paul said from the inverted fish box.

The three of them sat down to the chicken which Paul carved. Jessie noticed how hungry the two of them were. Soon the bird was stripped down to its breastbone, and both Sheila and Paul were now gnawing the legs in their fat-smeared fingers.

'This is wonderful meat,' Paul enthused. 'Is it one of your own?'

'Mrs Urquhart's, at the shop,' Jessie told them. 'She only feeds them on oatmeal, because she says that's what plumps up the breast.'

It was getting dark when Jessie left the house, but she had a torch in her jacket pocket. She found that she couldn't sleep, because she kept thinking of the two in the cosy cottage. They had a better life than her. They had freedom and faith, able to come and go as they pleased.

What did it mean to give oneself to Christ? Jessie wondered. It must be very different from giving oneself to the post office, lugging a heavy bag across the moor six days a week. She had never thought much about Christ before. Oh, he was always being mentioned at Sunday School, but Miss Brown the teacher hadn't made so much of the Son of God as Sheila and Paul did.

Two days later, Jessie informed her parents over breakfast that she had something to tell them.

'I'm going to move out of here.'

'Move out?' her father said uncomprehendingly, his knife poised above his black pudding.

'I'm going to live somewhere else.'

'You mean, you're moving to the mainland?' her mother said. 'I don't think that would be a good idea, dear. It's a very different place from this island. Postwomen get attacked there.'

'I'm not going to the mainland,' their daughter explained. 'I'm staying on the island.'

'I don't understand,' her mother said helplessly.

'I've met a couple and I want to join them in their mission.'

'What mission?' her father asked suspiciously, having laid down his knife and fork.

'A mission for Christ and the new age.'

'You've caught the *curam*,' her mother said in despair. 'They must be people from Lewis.'

'They're not from Lewis,' Jessie said, irritated by the prejudice. 'They're from the south and they're sincere people who want to spread the word.'

'Where are these wonderful people living?' her father wanted to know.

'In old Donald's house by the shore.'

He nodded. 'I've heard about them. They've run away from their partners and are living in sin. They're trying to ensnare you, lassie.'

'Ensnare me in what?' his daughter asked indignantly.

'In their wicked ways. I forbid you to go near that house again.'

'But I have to deliver their mail.'

'No you don't. You can leave the post office. Urquhart's looking for an assistant.'

'I don't want to work in a shop,' Jessie told her parents. 'I want to do something with my life – something worthwhile. The Lord gave me the mailbag for a purpose.'

'What do you mean, dear?' her mother asked anxiously, wondering if her daughter was having a particularly bad period.

'He gave me the mailbag so that I would deliver letters to Donald's house and meet Sheila and Paul.'

'It's Sheila and Paul, is it?' her father asked. 'How much time do you spend in that house?'

'That's my business,' Jessie said, rising from the table.

She moved out that night, taking a sleeping bag on her back

and two bags of provisions in her hands. They were waiting for her at the cottage, with a pot of whelks on the stove, and the table set for three, with a candle burning in the centre. As Jessie ate with them the house seemed to be more intimate and welcoming than her own.

'We saved this because we knew you were coming,' Paul said, producing a half bottle of whisky from the press.

'Why do you get messages?' Jessie asked after the warming dram.

'Because I'm the chosen one,' Sheila said with evident sincerity. 'The teachings which God gives to me, and to those he has chosen to help me, are in absolute accordance with the teachings of Jesus. Your name has been given to me in the messages. That's why I knew you had to come to stay with us, to continue the great work.'

After Paul had cleared away and washed the supper things, Sheila produced a Bible and read from it for an hour. Jessie hadn't listened so intently since childhood, when she had gone to Sunday School. In that small house, belonging to a mysterious man and lined with the gift of pine from the sea, Jessie experienced the power of Sheila. She read in a quiet voice, with conviction, as if she truly believed every word. Paul sat listening in the chair by the fire of sparking driftwood, his hands clasped.

At eleven Sheila closed the Bible and said that it was time for bed. Paul helped her to unroll her sleeping bag before saying goodnight and following Sheila into the other room. Jessie left her clothes over the back of a chair and lay on the uneven flagstones, her head turned to the dying fire. She thought of her bedroom at home, with its coombed ceilings, the familiar furniture, but she wasn't regretting her decision to give up her home comforts for this hard bed. The thought that she didn't have to rise in the dawn to fill her mailbag, then go out on the delivery made her contented. This was a new, more exciting way of life, and before she closed her eyes she said her prayers.

Next morning Paul cooked a pot of porridge, and then Sheila set out the day's work.

'Paul and I are going along the shore. You'll clean the house,' she instructed Jessie.

She was disappointed because she wanted to go with them, but as soon as they were out of the door she boiled a kettle on the stove and began to scrub at the sink with the bristled brush, but the marks wouldn't come out. She got down on her knees, the bristles hissing under her hand as she scrubbed the flagstones.

Two hours later Sheila and Paul came back. They had obviously been for a walk, because they didn't have the buckets for the whelks. Sheila ran her fingertips along the table.

'It isn't very clean.'

'I scrubbed it twice,' Jessie told her.

'I'm disappointed in you,' Sheila rebuked her. 'I thought you would try harder. If you're doing something for the Lord, it must be done perfectly.'

Jessie was close to tears as she scrubbed the table for the third time, and when Sheila came in again and tested it with her fingertips she said it was 'much better.'

Jessie had to make the lunch of saithe that Paul had caught off the rocks with a bamboo rod. Her parents wouldn't eat that fish, saying they were scavengers, but there was nothing else, and Jessie sat down to the meal, watching the other two picking the flesh from the skeleton with their fingers.

The two of them went out again in the afternoon, leaving Jessie with a new task: lugging two bags of whelks on her back a mile across the moor to the end of the road, where they would be collected by the van. By the time she got back it was dark, and Paul was preparing more fish for supper.

Afterwards they sat talking at the fire. Sheila explained that as a child she couldn't read the story of the crucifixion without bursting into tears.

'I had difficult parents,' she revealed. 'That was why I had a nervous breakdown at the age of ten. I lay in a darkened room, not wanting to eat, hoping that I would die. Then one night Christ in all his radiance came to me and told me to get up, because I would have work to do for him in the world. I didn't tell my parents about my vision. You know, Jessie, wanting Christ is like a constant gnawing pain at one's side, as if a nail has been driven in there. But you won't have experienced that.'

Jessie explained that she had been forced to go to the Free Church twice every Sunday, and had ended up hating it because of the coldness of the building and the harsh voice of the precentor leading the singing of the psalms.

'There was no music, no love,' she told Sheila and Paul as he threw another sod of peat on the fire.

'You'll find music and love through me,' Sheila promised.

She went next door and brought back a violin. As she put it under her chin and raised the bow Jessie thought that she was a beautiful woman. The Brahms concerto seemed to ring off the walls and to enter Jessie's heart.

'Sheila could have been a concert violinist,' Paul said. 'Except that the voice of Christ was stronger and sweeter than the sound of the strings.'

Sheila seemed more animated as she took her place by the fire again.

'We're going to found a movement,' she told the former post-woman. 'It will start here, in this cottage, and will go out to the world. Each night Paul and I pray that a wealthy patron will contact us and give us a substantial house. I know it's going to happen.'

'When you say a movement, what do you mean?' Jessie queried.

'A movement that will spread God's teachings. He gives me teachings which are in accordance with the teachings of Jesus. I have been chosen to spread this teaching. My movement will follow the teachings of the disciples. Each of us will live, either from the work of his or her hands, or on gifts from those who know that in the giving they are serving God and obeying his request to give.

You have been chosen to join our movement, Jessie, but you must obey me in everything. Today I set you two tasks, to clean this house and to take the whelks across the moor for collection. I am going to set you a third one now. I will sleep here and you will sleep with Paul next door.'

'I can't do that,' Jessie told them, horrified.

'Then if you can't, you don't have a place in our community,' Sheila said. 'We share everything, our bodies as well as food. It's all part of the love Christ speaks of and which he has chosen me to spread in the world.' She went to the door and held it open. 'You need to go tonight.'

Jessie could feel the cold wind blowing in from the moor, causing the fire to smoke. She had no torch to cross the dangerous moor with, and could end up in a bog. Why was Sheila doing this to her? Because she was going against her command. But Jessie sensed that this was also a test. If she went home to her strict father, a mother she couldn't discuss problems with, her life would resume its dull and unfulfilled routine, and she would end up a spinster with no experience of life and love. She hesitated in the draught from the open door because she had never had sex before. She had been warned often enough that the Free Church condemned it outside marriage, but this wasn't the Free Church. By the door, holding it open, was a beautiful woman who played the violin so well, who spoke so persuasively about her mission in life. She was asking Jessie to trust her, to join her mission. Who knows where it would lead?

Jessie got up and closed the door.

Paul was gentle with her that first time, and two nights later Sheila joined them, with him sleeping between them. Jessie felt more relaxed than at any time since she had arrived at the cottage, and did all the tasks that Sheila allotted to her, such as the cleaning. She even dug the latrine for the three of them on the moor while the other two collected whelks on the shore. In the evening after supper they would sit in silence while Sheila sat with a pad on her lap, writing down messages from God.

'He is pleased that you and Paul are together,' she read out to Jessie.

'Does he say anything about me visiting my parents?' Jessie asked anxiously, having not seen them for a month.

'I'll ask him,' Sheila said, closing her eyes, the pencil poised above the pad on her lap. Then she began to write.

'He says that you must cut off all connections with your family in order to do the great work that he has allotted to you through me.'

So Jessie stayed to scrub the flagstones, to fill in the latrine and open a new one, to sleep on one side of Paul, with Sheila on the other. Most nights he made love to both of them. Two months after she arrived Jessie was sick, and thought that the whelks of the previous night's supper must have been off. But Sheila had a message she had received in writing from the Lord.

'My disciple Jessie is pregnant by Paul. The child has been created with love and will be raised with love.'

Jessie was shocked at this revelation. How was she going to tell her parents? She wasn't, according to another message Sheila wrote down that night: 'Jessie must not tell her parents, because that will only cause trouble and strife.'

Jessie was miserable in her pregnancy, but Sheila made no allowance for her morning sickness, her increasing girth. She was still expected to scrub the floor, to fill in the latrine. At night she lay beside the father of the child now kicking inside her while Paul made love to Sheila. Jessie was beginning to wonder if she had made a terrible mistake, despite the reassuring messages that Sheila claimed were coming from the Lord.

'The baby is to be born here and delivered by us,' Sheila read out one evening when Jessie was so big that the chair wouldn't accommodate her.

'But suppose there are complications?' Jessie asked anxiously, having been told by her mother that her own birth had been difficult and dangerous.

This was when Sheila began to have some consideration for her, not allowing her to scrub the floor or to dig the latrine. Instead she was given the bed to herself, and the other two slept in the kitchen. On the night the contractions began Paul had a kettle of water boiling on the stove, and had scoured an enamel basin he had found on the shore. As she lay on the bed holding the father's hand Jessie had the impression that Sheila had done this kind of thing before.

Jessie loved her son, but two days later Sheila told her that she had to give up the baby to show her love for Christ.

'Why would Christ want me to do such a thing?' the mother asked tearfully.

'It's not for us to question his judgement,' Sheila said.

She took the baby for walks in her arms along the beach, and in the evening she and Paul lay with it between them while Jessie cried herself to sleep on the flagstones of the kitchen. She considered trying to run away with the baby, but Sheila was with the child all the time, and she couldn't get near it.

Jessie's father had driven all the way up to town in his Austin van because Archie Maclean was the person he trusted most on the island.

'Bella's ill with worry about Jessie,' he confided to the bank manager as he sat with a dram at the desk. 'We hear she's had a baby to that man.'

The banker was standing at the window, looking along Main Street.

'I've often wondered, Hector, why this island attracts so many deviants and chancers. Is it something in the air, or do they think that they can do here what they wouldn't get away with on the mainland? You say that these two have formed a religious sect and enticed your girl away?'

'How are we going to get her back, Archie?' his visitor asked in despair as he sipped the generous dram the banker had poured for the distraught parent. 'Bella was saying that it doesn't matter if the baby belongs to that man, we'll treat it as our own.'

'Leave it with me, Hector.'

That night when Gille Ruadh came up for his usual half bottle of whisky, the banker brought up the subject of the couple in the cottage at the other end of the island.

'What do you hear about them, John?' the banker asked.

The visitor was peeling the foil from the new packet of Gold Flake to offer the first one to the mistress of the bank house, and when he had brought her a light, and had one himself, he was able to talk.

'He sometimes phones from the box at the end of the road,' he confided to his host. 'I believe he's trying to persuade some wealthy woman on the mainland to buy a big house on the island so that he can start a sect. I don't like the sound of his voice.'

This was a tacit admission of what the island had long since suspected: the telephonist, his mother and his sister listened into calls. But Gille Ruadh knew that what he was saying would never go beyond that room above the bay.

'How do we get them off the island and Jessie McCabe and her child out of their clutches?' the banker asked his confidante.

'Well now,' Gille Ruadh said, picking a shard of golden tobacco from his lip. 'I could have words with a friend on one of the Sunday papers.'

The banker knew what this meant: the telephonist supplemented his income by sometimes selling stories to the newspapers.

A week later a reporter with a photographer parked their car at the end of the track and walked across the moor to the cottage. They met Sheila walking the baby in her arms by the shore.

'We heard about the sect you've formed here,' the reporter said. 'Can you tell us something about it?'

'I'm getting messages from Christ that I've to start a new movement.'

'Are you the Messiah?' the reporter enquired.

'Either that is true or I am the greatest blasphemer on this earth.'

'But how can you spread the word from a small cottage in the middle of nowhere?' the reporter wanted to know.

'Someone will come forward and give us the money to establish a community in much bigger premises.'

'How many of you are there?' the reporter asked.

'There are four of us, including this little fellow.'

'Can I speak with the other two?'

Sheila shouted for Paul and Jessie to come out. But it was Jessie the reporter wanted to speak with.

'Where do you come from?'

Jessie looked at Sheila, as if seeking permission to answer.

'From the island.'

'Why did you join these two?'

'Because I believe in their mission.'

'Are you the mother of the baby?' the reporter asked.

'Yes.'

'And who is the father?'

Again Jessie looked to Sheila, who answered:

'Paul is the father. This is a baby born out of absolute love for Christ.'

The reporter was writing all this down. Then he asked them to pose as a group against the background of the cottage, with Sheila in the middle with the baby. The reporter and the photographer accepted Paul's invitation to come into the cottage for tea.

The headline in the next Sunday's tabloid read:

FREE LOVE IN THE HEBRIDES

The reporter wrote how the three of them with the baby were living in a squalid cottage without proper sanitation and sharing a bed. That week the press pack descended on the island. They took up a position on the slope above the cottage, with their cameras.

'It's backfired on us,' Paul said. 'We'll have to leave.'

'Where are we going?' Jessie asked.

'To Glasgow,' Sheila told her. 'I had a message from the Lord last night.'

But Jessie didn't want to go to a dirty room in Glasgow. She lifted the baby from Sheila's arms, saying that the child needed changing, and then she walked out the door with her son and gave an interview to the waiting press, telling them that she was going home.

'You did well with these two down the island, John,' Archie Maclean said to Gille Ruadh. 'I had a call from Hector. They're delighted to have the girl and the baby home.'

'It was a good story,' the telephonist said, sipping his whisky.

5
The Saw Doctor

The saw doctor came regularly to the island, carrying his tools in a pigskin Gladstone, and with a long leather case in his other hand. He wore a soft brown hat with the brow snapped down over his thin intelligent face. Little was known about him for certain. It was said that he came from Glasgow, and had began to study medicine there, before running out of money. Having handled saws in the anatomy class, he had taken naturally to the trade. He travelled round the west of Scotland for most of the year, and though his charges were reasonable, it was thought that he made a decent living.

His first call after coming off the steamer was Neilly the butcher's on Main Street. He hung his soft hat on a hook from which a carcass was usually suspended, and picked up the saw that the butcher, a heavy drinker with a face the colour and texture of marbled meat, used on bone on the big wooden block. The saw doctor carried the instrument to the door and squinted along the blade as though he were aiming a rifle, his target the mansion house across the bay.

'What the hell have you been doing with this saw?' he called over his shoulder to the butcher. 'There's not a tooth in place.'

'I must have hit a bad piece of bone,' Neilly said, ashamed.

'A quality blade like this should go through bone easily. It looks as if you've been sawing through iron.'

'Can you save it?' the butcher asked anxiously, whose takings were transferred to the till of the Arms each night.

The saw doctor gave the butcher a contemptuous look as he swung the Gladstone up on to the block, snapping open the brass lock. He worked with pliers and files, straightening the teeth and sharpening them, then asking for a bone so that he could demonstrate the precision of his work. Every time he visited the island and straightened the teeth of this particular saw he had shown the butcher how to use it properly, and every time he came back – only an interval of three months – the teeth were out again.

'Look after it,' he told Neilly as he folded the ten shilling note into his waistcoat pocket and lifted his hat from the hook, but he knew that before the day was out the teeth would be crooked again.

The saw doctor then went along to the workshop of Munro the joiner. He was notoriously mean, saving bent nails from planks and straightening them as best he could, though he had ten thousand pounds on deposit in Archie Maclean's bank, and lucrative shares in a dozen companies. It was said of him that if he could have found a use for the sawdust on the floor, he would have done so. However, Munro knew that his livelihood and his reputation depended on the condition of his saws. A crooked or ragged end on a plank could cost him further work.

'I don't know what you do with these,' the saw doctor complained as he lifted them from the wall and carried them to the door to squint along them.

'It's the men, they're so bloody careless with them,' Munro countered.

'But most of your men have their own tools,' the saw doctor pointed out.

'Yes, but they use mine to save their own.'

'Every saw in this place is out,' the saw doctor pronounced.

It took him an hour with his pliers and a file to re-align and sharpen the teeth. Then he moved on to the planes, unscrewing the blades and locking them into the vice to sharpen them with another file, testing the edge with his thumb, but without drawing blood.

'That will be two pounds,' he announced when he had re-assembled the planes.

'That's more than the last time,' Munro complained.

'That's because the planes are in a worse state than last time,' the saw doctor informed him. 'With the state of these blades, it looks as if you've been trying to cut iron.'

'I don't need a lesson from you,' the master joiner rebuked him.

The saw doctor shrugged as he pocketed the two pounds.

'Suit yourself, but next time it'll be three pounds. I'm going to give you some advice which won't cost you anything, so no doubt you'll take it. Some of these planes and saws are so old that they look as if they were used to build Noah's Ark. Get rid of them. There are some very fine new tools on the market, with longer lasting blades.'

'I can't afford to replace these tools,' Munro complained. 'I'm barely making a living as it is.'

'You don't look like a man who's on the verge of starvation,' the saw doctor observed as he lifted his hat from the hook.

He walked up the brae to the Hebridean Hotel and went down the steps and through the tradesmen's entrance. The staff, and in particular the females, were always pleased to see the saw doctor, because they considered him to be a particularly attractive man. One of the maids, from the island of Tiree, thought he was the double of Douglas Fairbanks Junior, and at the end of the season, when she went home with a baby in her stomach as well as her bonus in her handbag, it was said that the saw doctor was the father.

One of the wits in the town said you could tell that because of the infant's perfect teeth.

Another maid, Effie, from the north of the island and dangerously overweight, brought him a cup of tea before he went up the lane to the hotel workshop, where he sharpened the saws that James the handyman used to try to keep the Victorian building up to standard, though the salt air ate into the window sills, and there was dry rot on the top floor, where the staff slept.

James was from Glasgow, and they discussed the appeal of that city as the saw doctor set the crooked teeth.

'I'm sorry I left Glasgow,' the handyman confessed.

'Why did you leave?' the saw doctor enquired as his little triangular file rasped against a tooth.

'I wanted fresh air and freedom.'

'Well you've certainly got both here.'

The saw doctor then took the path along the bay, across to the mansion house of the Ainsworthys, the shipping dynasty who had laid out the magnificent gardens of rhododendrons. An exotic leaf from a shrub found in the Himalayas drifted into the cleft of the saw doctor's hat, and there was pollen in the turn-ups of his corduroys.

He went down a perfumed path to a shed where Nicolson the head gardener was waiting for him, a selection of saws laid out for sharpening on a bench, from a cross-cut that took the strength of two men to use, to a small saw used for cutting back shrubs.

'People don't respect saws,' the doctor complained as he looked around for a place to hang his hat.

'I've got six men working here,' the head gardener reminded him. 'I can't be watching each one of them all of the time. Turn your back and something goes wrong. Last week I asked them to fell an old larch and what did they do? Brought it crashing down on one of the Colonel's finest rhododendrons, a bush the collector risked his life to get the seeds for.'

The saw doctor had balanced the end of the cross-cut on the bench and was squinting along the blade.

'Almost every tooth is out. And you tell me it cut down a tree. Are you sure it wasn't a concrete pole?'

The head gardener watched the saw doctor as he gripped the individual teeth with his pliers, straightening them, then squinting along the blade again. It was said that this man of few words had acquired Gaelic on his travels over the years, not least from the women he had bedded, but if you addressed him in that language, he looked at you blankly.

It took the saw doctor two hours to get the dozen saws on the bench to his satisfaction.

'You'll get paid up at the house as usual,' Nicolson told him as he lifted his hat from the peg.

The head gardener stood in the doorway of the shed, watching the saw doctor walking away with his Gladstone, convinced that there was more to him than met the eye, but what it was he couldn't say.

The housekeeper took the saw doctor into her office and handed over the ten pounds that the Colonel had left for his services.

'Would you like some tea?' she offered, and because he was too polite to tell her that he had had some already across at the Hebridean Hotel, he accepted a pot and a plate of cakes.

The housekeeper, who was in her forties, her black hair pulled back into a bun and fixed with pins that made it look painful, was fond of the saw doctor and sometimes dreamed about him. In one particularly vivid scene he had come into her room and hung his hat on the brass bedpost, and she had thrown back the covers for him.

'Don't you ever get tired of saws?' she asked.

'I love saws.'

'But nobody can love saws,' she said, puzzled.

'You can love saws in the same way as you can love a person. No, that's not quite accurate, because you can usually fix a saw, whereas some people are so out of tune that they can't be put back into it. It's like when you hear a saw going through wood and you know that it's not right.'

The housekeeper glanced at the clock.

'The Mistress will be ready for you now.'

All tradesmen took the back stairs, but he went up the front staircase. He seemed to be familiar with the layout of the house, because he turned along the corridor and knocked a door.

'Come in!' a voice sang.

'I'm so glad to see you again,' the attractive woman told him sincerely, taking his hat from his hand and laying it carefully on top of a bureau as if it were a Meissen plate she had just been presented with. The saw doctor was bending over a small machine on a table, testing the thin blade with a fingertip.

'The teeth are out,' he informed her, opening the Gladstone and taking out his tools.

'I made two jigsaws since you were last here,' she told him, and when he had finished adjusting and sharpening the tiny teeth she took him to another table in the window, where a jigsaw puzzle, perhaps a third completed, was spread out. It was a black and white view of the town across the bay, photographed by Mrs Ainsworthy, then pasted on to a board and cut into shapes by her with the saw he had just sharpened.

The saw doctor leaned over, selected a piece and completed the roof of one of the houses across the bay.

'I'm forgetting that you've been coming here for years,' she said. 'Shall we begin?'

The saw doctor knelt on the carpet and sprung the catches of the long leather case, lifting out an object and unwrapping the blue velvet covering to reveal a three feet long saw, of the kind carpenters use. He went to the chair in the other window, and she stood beside him as he put the handle of the saw between his knees and picked up the cello bow he had also brought in the long case.

Ten years before she had been staying in the Central Hotel in

Glasgow, having had a significant operation. Her husband had gone out for a meeting, and she was sitting alone in the lounge when she heard music. But it wasn't any instrument she could identify, so she had followed the melody down a long corridor, until she reached a saloon bar.

A man was sitting in a corner, playing a saw like a cello. She had sat, enchanted, because she had never heard of anyone coaxing music from a saw, and especially such haunting music, though the fashionable set drinking cocktails at the bar had paid no attention to the player.

At the end of the recital she had gone across to congratulate him, to be told that he came regularly to her island to sharpen saws.

'The next time you come, please play for me.'

The housekeeper was going through the hall when she heard the Mistress singing to the accompaniment of the saw. Though she had no French she understood the sentiments and began to sob:

> *'Plaisir d'amour ne dure qu'un moment*
> *chagrin d'amour dure toute la vie. . .'*

Up in the room the player bent the saw over his knee until it looked as if it would snap, or recoil and sever an artery in his arm with its ferocious teeth. But he understood saws and the bow swept on to the climax.

6
Sorcery

The woman who came down the gangway from the car ferry was wearing dark glasses and carrying a hammered aluminium case which flared in the sun like a mirror. She put her other baggage into the boot of the bus at the end of the pier, but took the metal case inside with her, her hand steadying it on the seat beside her as the vehicle took the turns and twists. Sometimes the road ran at sea level, with seals lying on skerries, and sometimes it climbed to cliffs where there were metal barriers.

The woman got off the bus outside the Arms, where she had reserved a room by phone. She carried the aluminium case up the stairs herself and locked the door before she went down to a dinner of prawns and summer pudding. Next morning she was waiting up at a cottage at the top of the town when a large van arrived, having crossed from the mainland on the first ferry. She supervised her furniture being carried inside because most of it was antique, a desk with inlay, a baby grand piano, its doleful hammers sounding as it was handled sideways through the narrow door into the low-ceilinged room with a view of the bay.

The woman was in her late thirties and attractive, with blonde hair that was thought to be natural, and large gold hoops hanging from her ears. There was speculation that she was a divorcee because there was a ring on her hand. Many people from broken love affairs came to the peace of the island to rebuild their lives, some of them taking on new identities. She didn't try to get a job in the town, so it was assumed that she had private means.

A fortnight after her arrival a sign appeared in the window of the post office.

AMANDA TREVELYN

AROMATHERAPIST

ARE YOU TENSE, STRESSED?

COME TO ME AND I WILL HELP YOU TO

RELAX!

James Mackinnon was a fisherman of twenty two and for two weeks he hadn't got one lobster in the six dozen creels he shot outside the sound. It made him depressed; he lay at home on the bed, smoking rolled cigarettes and wondering if he should go to the mainland for work. He was walking aimlessly round the top of the town when he noticed the card in the window of the cottage which had recently been sold.

'Can I help you?' the occupant asked as she came out.

'No, I was just reading the card,' he told her hastily.

'You're very nervous,' she informed him. 'You look as if you could do with some aromatherapy.'

'I don't know what that is,' he admitted.

'Come in and I'll give you a trial session.'

He hesitated before bowing his head to enter the low doorway, following her into the small sitting-room. A high narrow couch was covered with a white sheet, and the aluminium case lay on a round table, its lid up, full of small bottles fitted into compartments.

stories from an island

'Go behind that screen there and strip down to your pants,' she ordered him as she lit a candle in a glass bell. Flying cranes with stretched necks were painted on the screen. He came out in his Y-fronts.

'Face down,' she said, patting the couch.

He smelt the fragrance of the candle as she lifted little bottles from the case, shaking out drops into a phial.

'What do you fish for?' she asked as her soft palms smeared oil on his back.

'Lobsters.'

'I love lobsters. I used to eat a lot of lobsters in Cornwall. I'm a Celt like yourself, you see.'

'I'd bring you up a lobster, if I could get some,' he told her, beginning to enjoy the experience.

'You'll get them. I can feel your luck turning. Do you speak Gaelic?'

'Yes.'

'I want to learn it. I'm going to go to the night classes when they start. Your muscles are very tense; you need to relax. What do you do in your spare time?'

'I don't have much spare time,' he said. 'I've got the parents to look after. It's my father's boat I use. I fish for them too.'

'Surely a good-looking strong fellow like you has a girlfriend?'

'Not just now.'

'There now,' she said after twenty minutes. 'I'll not charge you this time. If you want more it's nine pounds for a half body, eighteen for a full body. I'd advise you to have treatment because your back's very tight. How about tomorrow night?'

The next day all his creels were full of lobsters, and one contained two, their claws locked in combat. He took the pair up to her in a pail that night.

'They're beauties,' she enthused as she put them into the sink. 'Is it a half or full body?'

'Full, please.'

He went behind the screen again to take off his clothes and lay on the couch as she mixed the oils. This time she pulled the waistband of his pants down, exposing his buttocks, and began to smear on the fragrance from the little pool in her palm.

'Relax,' she whispered as her hands slid up and down his back, kneading his buttocks.

He lived with his parents in a stone cottage his grandfather had built at the top of the town, in a street named after Queen Victoria, whose yacht had spent a night in the bay sheltering from a storm. The smell of the sea was always in his nostrils, but now he carried the scents of her oils about with him. The fragrances made him fall into a strange sleep in which he seemed to be still awake, as if her hands were under the bedclothes, massaging him. When he was out fishing the wind from the west seemed to be perfumed, and as he was hauling up the dripping cages he had the feeling that there was someone at his elbow.

He was going to her for treatment for his back every second night, but she wouldn't take any money for payment.

'We'll make a bargain. You teach me Gaelic and I won't charge you.'

'It could take a long time,' he warned her.

'That's all right, I've got all the time in the world.'

As he lay being massaged on the couch he taught her basic Gaelic conversation, correcting her pronunciation.

'What's that strange smell you bring in with you?' his mother asked as she set the table for his supper.

'It's the oil Miss Trevelyn uses on my back. It's doing me a lot of good.'

'Rubbish,' his father said. 'I had a bad back like you, and I lay on the floor for six months – aye, and went out fishing every day.'

'I wouldn't go near that woman,' his mother warned him. 'There were a few locals after that cottage, but she had more money. That's the way with this town now. If I hear Gaelic when I'm down at the shops I get such a surprise.'

He noticed that the oils seemed to get more pungent each time he went for treatment, and felt as if he were sliding away under her hands into another world of scents and brightness. One evening when he went up he found that a small table for two had been laid by the massage couch, a candle burning and the curtains drawn.

'We're going to have lobster for supper,' she told him.

'But how did you know I was going to bring any?' he asked in wonder.

'Because I'm psychic,' she said, taking the pail from him. She made him sit by the fire with a whisky while she put them into a pot.

'Do you believe that lobsters scream when they're being boiled?' she asked.

'It's an old wives' tale. It's only air escaping from the shell.'

When she brought through the scarlet creatures in a tureen the cutlery he picked up was fluted, solid silver, and the plates were old and valuable.

'I collect things,' she said, dishing out a vegetable he hadn't tasted before but which he found delicious. The lobsters were even better than the way his mother prepared them. He watched her breaking the claws to get at the meat.

'In what way are you psychic?' he asked.

'Because I know what's going to happen,' she told him.

'My grandmother was like that. She used to see lights in the cemetery when someone was going to die.'

'I see happier things,' the aromatherapist said. 'And I sometimes think I have the power to influence things. I hear you're a good singer.'

'Who told you that?' he asked, surprised, rolling a cigarette as she served him coffee in a little cup with a gold rim.

'I hear that you sing at ceilidhs. Give me a Gaelic song,' she asked.

'I'm not in the mood,' he said coyly.

'For my sake,' she pleaded.

He sat by the dancing flames, singing in his clear tenor voice a

Gaelic song about a woman lamenting a man who failed to return from the fishing.

'Why are so many Gaelic songs so sad?' she asked.

'I suppose it was because it was a hard life,' he said, though he had never thought about it before.

'Sing me a happy song,' she requested.

As he sang about two lovers lying on a flower-suffused machair in the summer she left the fire and was putting a lit candle into the little glass bell.

'You're sitting very stiff,' she told him. 'I think I'll give your back a massage. Get undressed.'

The fragrant candle was filling the small low-ceilinged room with its scent as he went behind the silk screen. He lay down on the couch and listened while the little bottles tinkled at the dresser.

'I'm going to use frankincense on you,' she said.

The aroma she was applying seemed to seep through his skin and reach his head immediately, as if he were intoxicated. She pulled down his pants and massaged his buttocks.

'Your sciatic nerve is still trapped,' she told him. 'Turn over.'

He must have fallen asleep because when he wakened she was standing naked by the dresser. She came with fragrances on her hands and began to massage his body until he seemed to slide away into another world, as if he were lying with her on a machair among aromatic flowers.

When he opened his eyes she was sitting by the fire with her clothes on. He didn't know if he had dreamed this experience which had left him so weak. Was it possible that he had made love to the woman? The luminous watch on his wrist showed one.

'I have to go home,' he told her. 'The parents will be wondering where I am.'

'Come tomorrow night,' she said dreamily.

She prepared carefully for this visit, studying her reference books at the good light at the window. She infused her pubic hair with sandalwood diluted in camellia oil and she made up a potion which included geranium, clary sage and yang yang to massage into her breasts. She mixed one drop of rose and one teaspoonful of camellia oil as a scented lip balm. The ritual was the same when he arrived. By the time he stepped out from behind the screen she was standing naked by the dresser. This time she climbed on top of him on the couch, her hair hanging over his face. He thought his heart was going to burst. He had been with girls before, but this was a new dimension.

He sang Gaelic songs as he raised the creels and removed the abundance of lobsters, but when he went home through the lanes after a session with her she seemed to follow him, and her scent filled his small bedroom as if she were in bed beside him. Even the moon looked more curvaceous in the skylight.

He was making so much money from the lobsters, he went to the mainland and bought a new car, a soft-top with wire wheels and a stereo. The other fishermen whose creels were empty were envious of him, and one of them came up to him in the pub.

'What's that smell?' he asked.

'It's the smell of success,' another fisherman said. 'That English woman up in old Sìne's house is giving him more than aromatherapy. I put in a bid for that place and lost it by thousands.'

'It's an open market,' Jimmy shrugged as he ordered a round.

'I don't want your dram,' the first fisherman told him, pushing away the glass.

'You're getting very thin,' his mother said. 'It's that woman you're going to for your back. I remember in the old days there was a woman called Kate Mhor who would put a spell on men to go with her, though she was no beauty.'

'My own brother fell for her,' her husband remembered. 'He told me himself that he found he was following her up through the lanes to her cottage. Look how thin he was when he died.'

The next evening, after he had sent four boxes of big lobsters away on the ferry for the London restaurant, Jimmy left his new car at his house and walked across to the aromatherapist's cottage with two lobsters in a pail, though his back was better. As he looked round from behind the screen she was standing naked by the dresser, massaging oils into her big breasts. The scents made him sway, as if he were drunk.

'I think you should put the lobsters on to cook,' he managed to call out.

'All right darling. Your treatment will take a while tonight.'

He knew he was in the grip of her spell, that she had used something on him which had put him in her power as well as bringing him a bounty of lobsters. He was the most successful fisherman on the island, with plenty of money in his pocket, but was losing all his friends and the respect of his parents, and none of the local girls wanted a spin in his new soft-top.

Still with his clothes on, he stepped out from behind the screen and picked up the poker. As he smashed the bottles she had been using on her breasts at the dresser the low-ceilinged room was full of pungent scents that made him reel, but he gave himself fresh air by breaking a window pane with the poker before smashing the remainder of the bottles in the aluminium case. The lobsters sounded as though they were screaming in pain as he went out.

7
The Winning Way

He sprang the catches of the case with his thumbs and unfolded the nightdress, holding it against his shoulders with his dark hands. She noticed how light his nails were, the colour of milk.

'Lovely for you,' he enthused, showing his white teeth. The nightdress had little ribbons dangling from the frilled neck.

'How much is it?'

'Six pounds seventy pence to you,' he said.

'It's too dear,' she complained.

He looked pained. 'You would pay three times that in a city store.'

She leaned over the table and touched the material which seemed to give her a shock.

'All right, I'll take it,' she said, reaching for her purse.

'What's the Gaelic for nightdress?' he asked.

She was so surprised by the question that she had to think.

'*Éideadh-oidhche.*'

She had to repeat it for him.

'*Eja*. It means clothing. And *oychu* is night.'

'*Éideadh-oidhche*,' he repeated solemnly. 'And this?' He took up one of the ribbons.

'*Ribean*. You see what an easy language Gaelic is.'

'Too difficult,' he said, shaking his head as he counted out her change. 'I know one word there's no Gaelic for.'

'What's that?' she asked.

'Me,' he said, touching his chest.

'*You?*'

'Pakistani,' he said.

'Oh but there is.'

He looked confused.

'*Seonaidh am Pacastannaidh*; Johnnie the Pakistani. That's what they call you.'

He showed his white teeth as he smiled.

'You'd better be going,' she urged him, looking at the clock, since her mother would be coming in soon. 'And don't forget my change.'

He put the coins in a little pile by her hand.

'I wish I could see you in your new *eja* – how do you say it?'

'*Eja-oychu*.'

She held open the door for him.

'*Oidhche mhath*.'

'What does that mean?'

'It means good night. I'll see you in a fortnight,' she reminded him.

'Oh aye, *oychu va*.' He turned at the door, gripping her hand. 'You take care,' he said earnestly.

She stood watching his old van bumping down the road. He had been coming to the house for two years, and she bought all her clothes from him because she was sorry for him. But she knew it was more than that as the vehicle disappeared over the rise of the hill. She stood on the step, arms folded, watching the light fade as she listened to the hasty pipe of an oystercatcher at the tide's edge. She was nearly thirty eight and had worked at the school dinners since she was sixteen. Having Gaelic hadn't done her any good. She should have gone to the mainland to get qualifications, but her mother was alone.

She was putting the kettle on when she heard the door, but it was too late to take the nightdress through to her bedroom. Her mother was a stout woman with a severe masculine face. Her legs spilled over her shoes, and she had a walking stick which she leaned on as if trying to force it into the ground.

'Is this you buying more trash from the *duine dubb*?'

She always referred to him as the 'black man'. She hooked her stick over the edge of the table and held up the nightdress against the glare of the light. 'Damned rubbish. You could spit peas through it. Oh I know where he gets his stuff all right.'

'How do you know?' her daughter asked aggressively as they faced each other over the table. They spoke Gaelic in the house, but most of it seemed to go into quarrels.

'I heard all about him at the Rural. He goes to the Barrows in Glasgow and fills his van up with trash that costs next to nothing, stuff that the big stores put out because there would be an outcry if they sold it. He brings it to this island because he thinks we're all fools. I worked in Glasgow as a girl and I know what good clothes are. Look at this; the label's been cut off it. Bri-nylon,' she said contemptuously. 'You want a good thick cotton to keep you warm in bed.'

'You've nothing better to do at the Rural than gossip,' Cathy said angrily.

'It would do you good to join and learn to make your own clothes instead of wasting your money on buying rubbish from the *duine dubb*. I don't like him, he's got a fly face. I hope you didn't give him tea because you'll have to scald the cup.'

'He hasn't got a disease. He's just the same as you and me.'

But her mother was taking off her coat and hat and sitting by the fire. She hated all foreigners because her husband had been killed on service in Korea – tortured first, she believed.

'I'll take a wee bit crowdie on a scone with my cup,' her mother said.

Cathy was so angry that the scone broke up under the pressure of the knife, and she had to throw it in the bin for the hens. She was going to end up looking after an old woman whose weight, moving her from the bed to the pan, would ruin her back. The nearest old folks' home was in the town in the north of the island, but her mother vowed she would never go into it.

There had once been a boy from Barra who had come in on a fishing boat. He was fair and quiet, and they had walked hand in hand by the shore. But her mother had deliberately used Gaelic dialect words he didn't know, and he hadn't come back.

Cathy went through to her bedroom and undressed. She put on the new nightdress, standing in front of the mirror, arranging the ribbons at her throat, twirling round as she had seen the models from Paris doing on the television. It was very pretty, and she felt warm and comforted in bed.

The next night Johnnie was due, her mother was out again at the Rural.

'How did the *eja-oychu* fit?' he asked.

She was very impressed that he had remembered the Gaelic.

'It's very nice,' she said, but didn't tell him of the dreams she had when she wore it.

This time he had brought her a white blouse with a Peter Pan collar, and he held it in front of her, without touching her breasts.

'Beautiful,' he said.

He had such white bits to his eyes, such a ready smile, and she liked his full lips.

'Where do you get your stuff?'

He put up his palms, waving them like the Black and White Minstrels on the television. 'Only the very best,' he said earnestly. 'No rubbish. This blouse would be fifteen pounds in Glasgow. For you, five,' he added, folding the sleeves tenderly over the garment.

She paid him, then asked him if he would like a cup of tea.

'Now how do you say that in Gaelic?'

She was touched because she knew that he was showing interest in Gaelic for her sake. He held the white scone in his dark hand, biting into the crowdie she had made herself.

'You'll have to go,' she advised him. 'I have to practise.'

'Practise?'

'For the local Mod.'

'Mod?' he asked, puzzled.

'It's a kind of Gaelic festival we have every year. I sing at it.'

'Sing for me.'

She was embarrassed, but she stood, her hands clasped, singing the lullaby her mother had used when she was young, a song she had never heard anyone else sing and which she hoped to win the silver medal with, after all those years of trying.

'You teach me,' he asked, and she went over it with him, line by line. He stood beside her, singing with her. The inside of his mouth was pink and his voice was soft.

'What's love in Gaelic?' he enquired when they were having tea.

'It depends what kind of love you mean.'

He put his hand on his heart.

'*Gaol*,' she said.

'*Gul*,' he repeated solemnly. The depth of the word seemed to suit his husky throat. 'And how do you say my love?'

She blushed.

'You're making a fool of me.'

'No, no,' he assured her, taking her hand.

'*Mo ghaol*.'

'*Mo gul*,' he repeated, looking into her eyes.

This time she put the blouse through in the bedroom before her mother came home from the Rural.

'The walk's getting too much for my legs,' the old woman

complained. 'I'll have to give it up.'

'It's good for you, getting out,' her daughter said, alarmed because Johnnie wouldn't call again if she were at home.

'What have you been doing all night?' her mother asked, looking around suspiciously.

But she had washed and dried the cups.

'I was practising for the Mod.'

'I'll listen to your song before I go to bed,' the old woman said.

Cathy stood by the table, linking her fingers and moving her arms, the way her mother had showed her.

'Aye, you've fairly come on, you should win it this year,' her mother gave her a rare compliment. She herself had won the silver medal fifty years before.

The blouse fitted so well over her breasts, and the collar was so neat, the way it lay against her throat, she decided to wear it for the Mod. She was happier at her work, singing as she diced the vegetables for the broth in the school kitchen, stirring the custard for the children. It was raining the day Johnnie was due.

'I won't go to the Rural tonight,' her mother said. 'The rain's got into my bones.'

Cathy went down the road to the box and phoned the neighbour, asking her to call and offer her mother a lift, though she wasn't to say Cathy had phoned.

'*Mo ghaol,*' Johnnie greeted her.

When she saw what he was lifting out of his case she could feel the heat in her face. His dark fingers were inside the stretched knickers, the way the X-ray had looked when she had hurt her hand in the school kitchen and had had to go to the hospital on the mainland.

'Lovely on you,' he said.

'Don't be dirty,' she said, though it was making her feel queer.

'What's the Gaelic for knickers?' he asked.

'It's a secret word,' she said.

'Tell me.'

She hesitated. '*Drathars*.'

He repeated it.

'What's love-making?' he wanted to know, still holding the stretched knickers.

'*Suirghe*.'

It was a word she hadn't used before, but somehow she knew it. He repeated it.

'These knickers are specially for you. I only got one pair in Glasgow. They were ten pounds; for you, three.'

They had a little red bow on the front, and when she touched them they seemed to give off an electric shock that ran like lightning through her bones.

'You'd better go,' she urged him.

'No tea?' he asked mournfully.

'Not tonight. Next time you come I'll have something special.'

'*Mo ghaol*,' he said on the step, kissing her cheek.

She heard his van going away. Then five minutes later it came back. She went to the door, but it was her mother getting helped out of the neighbour's car.

'We passed the *duine dubh* on the road,' she said accusingly. Then she saw the knickers on the table. She snatched them up and ripped them apart between her fists, throwing them on the fire.

'The *duine dubh's* never setting foot in this house again.'

'Then I'll go.'

'*You* go?' her mother said, rounding on her with her angry precise Gaelic. 'And where would you go? Do you realise what it costs to put a roof over your head, and you earning so little at the school meals? I don't charge you rent; all I ask is a bit of civility and obedience. You know I don't like that black bugger in this house. Giving you these *drathars* shows the dirty trash of a man he is.' The way she pronounced it, she made the word *drathars* sound so ugly.

The night Johnnie was due she made an excuse that she wanted a walk, but she waited at the road end till it got dark.

A fortnight later they took the bus to the town so that her mother could get elastic stockings and have her hair done. Cathy went off by herself and saw a big unfamiliar van parked on the old pier by the clock. When she went round to look she read the new lettering on the side, painted over old words she couldn't make out.

SEONAIDH: AODACH
(Johnnie: Clothing)

The sliding door was open, and he was at the counter, talking to a stout woman. Cathy lingered at the bottom of the steps, waiting to speak to him by himself. So this was why he hadn't come to the house the last time: what a lovely surprise, setting up a mobile shop on the island. He should do very well.

His dark hands held the nightdress with the ribbons against the woman.

'*Se stuth anabarrach math a tha an seo. Agus innsidh mi seo dhut bu toigh leam d'fhaicinn 'se ort, ach dh'fheumainn a dhol a mach air an uinneig nuair a thigeadh do dhuine a stigh.*'

('This is very fine material. I'll tell you this, I wish I could see you in it, but I would have to get out of the window when your husband comes in.')

Cathy couldn't believe her ears. How could he have picked up such fluent Gaelic from his visits to her? Then she understood. He had been going round the doors of other women, getting Gaelic from them as well. The fly bugger. But she wasn't angry with him; it was because he wanted to come and live on the island, to be near her, so that he could speak her native language with her.

Blushing at his Gaelic patter, the stout woman bought the nightdress and came out. Cathy took a deep breath before going up the steps, as she had done before she had gone up on to the Mod platform to sing the lullaby. She had worn the Peter Pan blouse he had brought for her, and as she crooned the song her Gaelic had seemed to come as a new language from deep within her. It had felt as if there were a real baby in her rocking arms.

Cathy climbed into the van. His back was to her at the counter as she arranged the Peter Pan collar to show the silver Mod medal at her throat. She was about to greet him in Gaelic when a woman came up the steps. Her head was draped in fine translucent material, and there was a pearl at the side of her nose. Johnnie leaned over the counter and began to sing to the baby the woman was carrying. It was the Gaelic lullaby her mother had sung to Cathy, and he sang it fluently and with feeling in his soft voice as the dark woman rocked the child in her arms.

Cathy stood among the rails of cheap clothes with the labels cut out. She felt naked. It was worse than being raped. If he'd taken that part of her by force, it couldn't have hurt so much. But he'd taken the Gaelic lullaby, the secret song that contained the only tenderness that her mother had ever shown towards her, and he'd coaxed it out of her for the baby he already had by a woman of his own race. The silver of the medal was cold and heavy on its chain against her throat as she went down the steps of the van, across Main Street to the hairdressers where her mother was dozing under the drier.

8
Chains

'It'll soon be the blind whist,' Katie used to say. The word was so mysterious, like a whisper, and it wasn't until she was in her teens that Marsaili understood that her aunt was referring to a card game.

Every autumn Katie arranged a whist drive in the hall and sent the proceeds to a home for blind ex-servicemen on the mainland. Marsaili helped her to set up the green baize card tables, to put out the decks of cards and the ashtrays. On the night the canvas seats of the tubular chairs sagged with about forty backsides. Most of the players were elderly, but Katie was the best player in the town, if not on the island.

Her brother the banker used to say that she would have made a fortune as a professional gambler, and Marsaili pictured her glamorous aunt sitting in a saloon among men, as in a Western film, with a cigarette jutting from the corner of her mouth, and a hand that would sweep the winnings her way. She might even have had a celluloid shade over her eyes, to protect them from the glare of the kerosene lamp above the table; and very likely there would have been a little silver revolver stuck in her garter.

The whist drive was held in the hall, which had been built for the townspeople by Ainsworthy the shipping magnate, whose mansion, embowered in imported exotic plants, was across the bay. The hall was now half a century old, and badly needed a new staircase and more than a lick of paint.

Katie wore an elegant dress and one of the innumerable gold chains that she had acquired in her profession as an antiques dealer. She had learnt the trade from books and from experience, attending sales the length and breadth of the island, training her eye to distinguish between what was re-saleable, and what was trash.

At the whist her table always won, and at the end of the night she announced the proceeds and handed the cheque to the man in dark glasses, with medals on his chest, who had come from the home on the mainland.

At a whist – for the Lifeboats – Katie suddenly couldn't see the cards in her hands, but didn't cry out in fright. 'Excuse me,' she said, calmly, and laid the cards on the baize. 'Would you take my place?' she asked one of the women serving the tea.

Dr Murdoch shone a slim torch into Katie's eyes.

'It was like a small receding sun,' she said, describing the experience to her brother Archie.

'You'll have to go to see a specialist on the mainland,' the doctor told her, and sat down to write a letter she had to take with her.

Her brother went on the train with her to Glasgow and waited until she came out of her appointment at the eye infirmary.

'Well, Archie, my eyes are deteriorating,' she told him.

'What disease is it?' he asked.

'They didn't put a name to it and I didn't ask. I told the specialist what a problem it was going to be, because I need a jeweller's glass to check the hallmarks on the pieces of silver that are brought to me, not all for sale, some for valuation, so I have to be accurate. A year can make a big difference in value.'

'You can afford to retire,' Archie told his sister – or at least, that was what Marsaili heard him reporting to her mother when he arrived home. 'I told her, you've got a house full of valuable things. And you're not short of money.' The previous week she had paid five thousand into her account, the proceeds of a Peploe painting of Iona she had paid two thousand for. But the banker couldn't discuss his sister's finances with his family because of confidentiality.

Three days later Katie came upstairs to the bank house with a letter to show her sister-in-law.

'Isn't it sad, to be registered partially sighted?' she said.

'It's just a term,' Alice, always the soothing one, reassured her.

But two days later Katie was back.

'Just look what I received in the post this morning. A folding white cane, and a clock that actually talks to me. I don't need that,' Katie told Alice indignantly. 'I've got a grandfather clock in my hall, made in Perth around 1800, that delivers the sweetest chimes I can hear at the top of the house.'

'They mean well,' her sister-in-law told her.

But it was obvious that Katie's eyes were getting worse. It was reported to Alice that in the Co-operative her sister-in-law couldn't locate her favourite ice cream in the deep freeze cabinet and had to call an assistant across, though the flavour (chocolate) was just beside her hand.

'I will never use a white stick,' she vowed to her brother.

When old people died in the town, their relatives or lawyers usually called in Katie to do a valuation of the contents of the house. She would enter a room, sweep her experienced eye around it, and value the furniture to the nearest hundred pounds. One day she went to the sale of the contents of a mansion house in the south of the island. The owners, a retired Colonel and his wife, were having to sell up because he had squandered her fortune on gin, and was also deeply in debt to a mainland bank which refused to wait for his death (he had cirrhosis) so that they could realise the security of his considerable life insurance policies.

The steamer was late that day because of bad weather, so the dealers from the mainland didn't get to the sale until it was almost over. With hardly anyone bidding against her, Katie bought many elegant pieces of furniture that day, including an escritoire with a secret drawer in which she discovered a pearl necklace. She speculated that the wife of the alcoholic Colonel might have hidden this last item of her precious jewellery to prevent him from sending it to London for sale and converting the proceeds into drink.

Katie was honest as well as shrewd, and asked the woman if these were her pearls.

'How much are they worth?' she asked Katie.

'They're river pearls, but not the best quality. About five hundred, I should say.'

'Give me the money in cash,' the desperate woman pleaded. 'But don't let that drunken bastard see. The money will take me abroad to start a new life.'

Katie got one thousand pounds from a city dealer for these same pearls, and with all the furniture, including the elegant escritoire, she tripled her investment when items were taken away to be auctioned in Glasgow.

One afternoon Katie went to value the contents of Mrs Mor Macdonald's house, a substantial villa in its own grounds at the top of the town. She went round the rooms and at the end she told the lawyer the entire contents were worth three thousand pounds.

'I hope you'll buy the lot,' he said, relieved at being spared the trouble of disposing of the contents.

Katie wrote him a cheque, and the van duly came from the mainland, but the stuff only fetched a thousand at auction.

'Maybe you overlooked something,' Alice said kindly, knowing it was her sister-in-law's deteriorating eyes that had caused the over-valuation. 'I know you love beautiful things, Katie, and you've seen your share of them in your time, but you should take it easy now and enjoy yourself.'

'You mean, give up the business?' Katie asked.

'It would be for the best,' her sister-in-law advised.

This time three vans came from the mainland to take away Katie's stock, but no one ever heard what she got for the things at auction, though Alice was told by a third party that a Regency sideboard Katie had found covered in bird droppings in an out-house down the island had fetched three thousand guineas.

Katie's eyes were worsening quickly. She was lucky to step out of her car with only a laddered stocking the day she drove it into a wall, claiming that she was only moving the car out of the way. Archie sold the car for her, and reminded her that she had enough money to take taxis up and down the hill.

Marsaili met her aunt one afternoon on the middle brae. She couldn't have seen her niece coming, because she was using the white cane, swinging it in front of her as she descended in her unsuitable shoes. Marsaili seriously thought about passing her without acknowledgement, letting her go on down alone with her white wand to the hairdressers for her weekly perm, but the girl spoke up.

'Is that you, Marsaili? Now I want you to do a big favour for me, and if you do it I'll give you a silk blouse I bought for myself some years ago and have never worn and which will fit you perfectly. Will you do it?'

'It depends what it is, auntie Katie.'

'Please don't tell your parents – or anyone else for that matter – that you met me with a white stick.'

It was an easy promise to keep on Marsaili's part, though she didn't get the silk blouse. The next time she saw her aunt she was with a man, and he was taking her arm down the brae. She didn't see her niece, and on that occasion Marsaili felt able to report the sighting to her parents.

'Describe this person,' Archie asked his daughter.

'Small. Elderly. Very well dressed in a double–breasted suit, with a hat. Oh yes, and he had a moustache.'

'It's nobody I can think of locally,' Alice pondered. 'I wonder who Katie's friend is?'

A week later the banker came upstairs with news.

'I found out about the fellow who was with my sister. He's a dealer from the mainland. Apparently he specialises in gold.'

'Did Katie tell you this, Archie?' Alice asked in surprise.

'Katie tells me nothing. Carmichael in the Arms told me. The man's staying there. His name is Finnegan.'

'He sounds Irish,' Alice said.

'I understand that Katie has dinner with him every night in the hotel,' her brother said disapprovingly. 'It sounds to me that this Finnegan fellow has got himself a good catch. It's easy for him to carry out a valuation: he only needs to price the gold chains round her neck to know he's on to a winner. And I thought my sister had a shrewd head on her.'

Marsaili saw Katie and Mr Finnegan walking arm in arm several times when she was up at the top of the town, visiting friends. Either she couldn't see her niece or she didn't want to acknowledge her. Katie went to one of the summer ceilidhs with him, sitting very prominently in the front row, his hat under his chair. Marsaili observed this when she was up on the platform, dancing the Highland Fling.

'There's going to be a match there,' Archie Maclean observed over a supper of crabs. 'Mr Finnegan has got the grip of my silly sister. He's taken advantage of her because of her eyes.'

One evening Katie phoned her sister-in-law.

'I'm going away for a spell, Alice. Perhaps Archie could keep an eye on the house, since I still have some valuables here.'

'Did she say where she was going?' Archie asked.

'No, and it wasn't my business to enquire,' Alice said.

'When she comes back she'll be Mrs Finnegan – minus the gold chains,' her brother predicted.

'Katie has asked me to take over the running of the blind whist,' Alice announced to her family. 'I'm happy to do it for such a worthy cause.'

It was the week after Katie had gone away. Marsaili helped her mother to set out the green baize tables, the decks of cards, the ashtrays and the books of matches with a Christian message on them. There was a full house that night, and at the end the banker's wife, elegant in a tweed costume with an Iona brooch on the lapel, handed over a cheque for a record amount to the blind man with the medals.

'In thanking you all for your continued generosity, I want especially to thank Katie, who unfortunately can't be with us tonight,' the man said in a little speech he made from the platform, where Alice guided him on her arm. 'Over the years she has raised many thousands of pounds for our home, and we have many comforts because of her and your kindness.'

Two days later Katie came back. It was a dramatic moment that will live in the annals of the town where there is a lot of coming-and-going now, especially in summer. Katie came off the late bus at the memorial clock, but she was not alone. That is not to say that she was accompanied by a male friend. She had been widowed for years, and though she fluttered her eyes at men, no one knew how serious it was.

Katie had a dog with her. A guide dog. In a yellow harness. And she had on a yellow armband. It was a golden retriever, a beautiful creature with such expressive eyes.

'Sit,' she said, and the dog sat on the pavement until the pneumatic door of the bus had closed and it was safe to cross.

Marsaili was sitting at the clock with her friends, teenagers looking for romance on a balmy night when she saw her aunt being helped from the bus. She crossed the street to her.

'She's so beautiful,' Marsaili said, fondling the retriever's soft ears.

'*She* is a *he*,' Katie corrected her niece. 'And his name is Sandy. I didn't choose it; it's the name given to him by the man who runs the training school for blind dogs and who gave me a week's course in handling it. Sandy will be my eyes from now on.'

'Will I walk you up the brae?' Marsaili asked.

'No need,' her aunt said lightly. 'Sandy and I will take it easy so that he can get used to this place.'

Archie Maclean became very fond of that dog and used to feed it bits of biscuit when his sister called.

'I wonder what happened to Mr Finnegan,' he asked one night.

'Katie was talking about him this afternoon,' Alice revealed.

'Was she?' he said, surprised. 'Come on, Alice; give us the low-down on him. He stole one of her gold chains.'

'No he didn't, Archie. In fact he bought her one, and though she couldn't see it, she knew by the feel that it was real gold. It turned into a choice between him and the dog.'

'Sometimes you're not easy to follow, Alice,' the banker said wearily.

'You're too impatient to hear the end of a story, Archie. Because she's blind Katie needs someone to take her about. You know that your sister is cute. I suppose she had to be, as an antiques dealer. Katie always knew how to bid.'

'So what was her offer to Mr Finnegan?' her brother wanted to know.

'She was waiting for Mr Finnegan to make the move. Oh, he was amorous enough, if you know what I mean, but Katie wanted a commitment, and he wouldn't give her one. "He didn't value me as I should be valued" – that's what she said to me.'

9
The Man from the Sea

On the Sunday morning of the declaration the accumulator was almost flat because she had been listening to Gaelic choirs that week. She put her ear to the cloth panel of the wireless, but the only word she could make out was war.

Seònaid Eachainn Fhionnlaigh decided not to carry the accumulator through the rocks to the township the next day to have it recharged overnight in the back room of the shop. Her only brother had been killed on the Somme, and men were beasts who fought over things that weren't worth fighting for. She didn't need the wireless; she had plenty of songs herself.

Her croft on the headland was called *taigh cùil an t-saimh*, the house at the back of the ocean. The five acres were fertile and had been worked by her family for more generations that she could count back. Both her parents had been carried through the rocks to the township cemetery. After the earth had settled a mason had come from the mainland to carve their names and essential dates in a plain style, and she had paid him in old notes that her father had got for a cow whose calf was long since dead.

She was considered to have strange powers by others on the island. When she was eight there had been an exceptional frost which had made the ground heave. A stone wall on her way to school had tumbled, and in the debris of plants and stones she had found a dozen frozen small birds. They were *clacharan* (wheatears) which should have been in a warm land far in the south. She had taken them to school in her hat, but the teacher had ordered her to put them outside in the bin until the ground thawed and they could be buried.

But Seònaid had knelt in front of the fire and laid out the birds with their stiff feathers and claws, as if they were made of stone. After a few minutes one of them had opened an eye, and another had twitched. They came slowly to life, shaking their heads and lifting their wings from their bodies. The teacher said it was witchcraft and belted Seònaid. She took six strokes while the *clacharan* fluttered on the hearth, then placed the birds back in her hat and put it on her head to keep them warm. She kept them in a box by the fire, feeding them with her fingers till the better weather came.

She didn't leave school; she stayed away for so long that they took her name off the register. First her mother died, peacefully, at her spinning wheel without the thread breaking. Then her father took pains in his chest, as if a wire was being tightened around him. She nursed him until one afternoon a golden butterfly came in the open window, fluttering round the sick man's face. It was a *dealan-dé*, the fire of God, and it flew out of the window with his soul. Her parents left her four pounds ten shillings in cash and a hundred songs.

She had plenty to do, working the croft. Since she had taken her father's name she didn't see why she shouldn't also wear his boots. She cut her own peats and carried them across the rocks on her back to the stack beside her house. She had reroofed it herself in corrugated iron, and never lost a sheet in a gale, though the headland was so exposed. After big storms she would see strange birds. Once a big white bird the size of four seagulls had soared for a day above the headland, but in the morning it was gone with the turned wind.

She did her own ploughing, and men climbed a hill on the island to see the straightness of her furrows. She had no running water in the house, but the well had never been known to run dry, even in the great frost of the *clacharan*. She was content with her own company, sitting on the plank with the hole in the *tigh beag* for as long as she wanted, with the door open on hot days, listening to bees in the clover.

Once a fisherman had sheltered from a storm in the bay below her croft. She had made him broth from her own mutton with vegetables she dug up herself, but the weather didn't lift that night and in a moment of defencelessness she had allowed him into her bed. The experience was not as satisfying as her body had promised when she was a girl, so she decided to remain by herself.

They were always talking about the war in the shop, and how short things were getting. But she made her purchases quickly and didn't join in the conversation, though everyone wanted to talk to her because of the pleasure of hearing her Gaelic. It was different, purer than that spoken in the rest of the island. It had the colour and sharpness of the first tangerines that had arrived on the island. She was also known to have songs that no one else had, as if the headland were a separate place in the ocean. But though she had a fine voice that made people stop work a mile off on a still day as she swung the scythe, she refused to sing at ceilidhs. She didn't go to church, and when the minister cycled through the rocks to ask her if she had the comfort of prayer at least, she told him it was none of his business.

'You should join the WRNS, Seònaid Eachainn Fhionnlaigh,' Urquhart the shopkeeper said to her as he counted up her purchases too quickly for her liking.

'What's that?' she asked suspiciously.

'It's the women's navy,' he told her, conscious that he had an audience. 'You're a big strong woman, good in a boat.'

'And why are you not at the war yourself, since you know so much?' she demanded, while the women pushed forward to hear her Gaelic.

'Because this shop has to stay open,' he said.

She had kept her father's boat and varnished it every Spring. One evening she was out fishing for mackerel, hauling them aboard on the line of feathered hooks when she saw the warship passing. It was huge, with long guns, and it rocked her boat so much that she rowed for the shore, trailing fish on the line. But the warship dropped anchor in her sleep and stayed for several days until she took an infusion of nettle tea.

Bodies were being washed up on the island from ships torpedoed in the convoys. As they were buried in the hillside cemetery she could hear the prayers being said on still days as she worked in her fields beside the blue sea, singing Gaelic songs that she would never pass on to anyone else because they were more precious to her than what she had given the storm-bound fisherman.

She was gathering seaweed for her fields when she saw the object in the water. At first she thought it was a sack. Over the years the sea had brought her many useful things, ropes to secure her haystacks against the winds, pieces of fishing net to put round the chicken coop, and spars of wood for a shed whose roof arrived a year later on a Spring tide. But this time when she waded out she found a corpse. He was wearing a dark blue-grey boiler suit and when she turned him over she saw a head clad in a leather helmet open at the ears, and two eyes staring at her from the salt-streaked goggles. She knew that she should have gone straight away to Farquhar the special constable to report the body but instead she lifted it into the wheelbarrow and trundled it up to the croft, tipping it off carefully and propping it against the stall in the byre. She sat on her milking stool, her knees spread, studying him. The goggled eyes seemed to stare back at her.

That night she dreamed that she was sitting beside him in a plane as they passed over the island, and she could see distinctly the township and faces that she knew turned up to look at her. People were waving but she didn't wave back because her family had always kept to themselves.

The next morning when she went out to the byre she found that one of his fingers had been chewed by a rat, so the next night she put the cat in with him to watch him. When she came in the next morning the animal was curled up beside him.

She continued to have dreams, and on one occasion flew with him to Ireland and saw the Giant's Causeway, which she had only ever seen on a postcard. When she was sitting milking the cow she got into the habit of talking to the airman in Gaelic, her sentences constructed as if she were receiving a reply. One evening after she had made a cheese she touched the zip on the pocket above his heart, but it wasn't until two days later that she opened it.

It contained a mouth organ, with a blue bird lacquered on the metalwork. It was curved to the mouth but when she tried it she swallowed the Atlantic. She took the instrument inside and put it to dry on the shelf above the stove. The next night she put it to her mouth again, but it made a mournful sound that frightened her, so she went out and returned it to his pocket.

She opened the other pocket and found a wallet. She took it into the stove and dried it, then spread the snapshots on the oilcloth of the table, beside the lamp. There was a picture of a wooden house with a balcony, and a mountain behind it with snow. A woman was standing, wearing an apron printed with flowers. Seònaid Eachainn Fhionnlaigh took the lamp and photograph out to the byre, setting it down on the ground and comparing the face in the photograph with his. It must be his mother or sister. She took the photograph back in and soon her imagination had allowed her to enter the wooden house. She heard her heels on bare floors and saw plain furniture like the kind she had in the croft. There was a table set, and she sat down and ate a strange strong sausage, drinking beer from a tall elaborate jug with a handle you held down with the thumb. Afterwards she went up wooden stairs to a bed which had a pillow filled with goose feathers on which she slept soundly.

It was a hot summer. The cow was reluctant to go into the byre when she brought it in in the evening, its udders trailing through the flowers. When she sat on the stool milking she sang to the German airman. She opened his collar at the neck as if to give him more air. There was an iron cross round it. That night she flew with him to the Long Island to visit a cousin she didn't know she had, and was given a strange cheese.

When she went down to the shop she heard about an attack on a convoy that had taken place.

'A plane appeared out of the clouds and started bombing one of the ships,' Urquhart said. 'There was a destroyer escorting it, and it fired at the plane. They were sure they hit it, because it didn't come back.'

'I thought I heard a plane the other night,' one of the women said.

'Did you hear anything on the headland, Seònaid Eachainn Fhionnlaigh?' the shopkeeper asked.

She shook her head and passed the can across for a gallon of paraffin for her lamp.

'The only good German's a dead German,' Urquhart said vehemently as he went into the back shop. When he came back with the can she unscrewed the cap and stuck her finger in to make sure that she was getting the full measure.

One afternoon she went along to the shop for salt to cure some herring she had caught, but it was locked, with several women gathered outside.

'He got a telegram last night,' one of them explained to Seònaid. 'His son was shot down over Germany. They say he's missing, but Urquhart's sure that he's dead. It's a terrible thing, when there's only the one child.'

There was a bad smell in the byre now and the cat wouldn't stay with him at night. He would have to be laid to rest. She dug beside the cow she had buried a month before. On a blue morning she lifted him into the wheelbarrow. She laid him down, still wearing his goggles, and sang him a Gaelic song she had heard at her mother's knee as she put the earth back gently.

For nights she couldn't sleep for the droning of a plane she could not see, but which came and went, like an insect in a dark room. She opened the curtains and saw a shooting star.

In the Spring she made a hole with her finger in the grave and planted daffodil bulbs she had dug up from the front of the croft. She had kept his leather helmet, and wore it while she worked the land. On the night of the bombing of Hiroshima she was mucking out the henhouse when she suddenly decided to get the accumulator charged because she would like to hear a Gaelic choir again.

10
The Cave of Gold

'Try the first verse again,' her mother said.

Cairistiona stood, composing herself, her hands together.

'Is truagh mi rìgh gun tri làmhan,
Da làimh 'sa phìob, da làimh 'sa phìob. . .'

My sorrow that I don't have three hands,
Two for the pipes, two for the pipes,
My sorrow that I don't have three hands,
Two for the pipes, one for the sword.

Her father was sitting with a leg over the arm of his chair, watching her. She kept her eyes on his dangling cigarette as she sang.

'That was much better, wasn't it, Neil?' her mother said. 'You're going to win it, pet.'

She was nine years old and was entering the medal competition in the island Mod with *Uamh an Òir*, 'The Cave of Gold', the tune her mother used to hum to her as she was putting her to bed.

'I learnt it from my mother. It's about a piper who gets a silver chanter from a beautiful girl who plays the harp. I'll teach you the song one day.'

Cairistiona liked to fall asleep listening to her mother humming the song. She dreamt of a cave with a dazzling opening in the darkness. Inside was a bicycle made of gold, with a little pouch hanging from the saddle.

Her mother had been a good singer, and they said that her daughter had inherited her voice. But she had never heard her father sing. He came from an island further north, and his Gaelic had strange harsh words. Some nights she heard her parents quarrelling in the bedroom, and once something had hit the wall.

The croft was isolated and she had to play by herself, going up and down the rough road with her doll in the pram. On the nights when her mother was out at the Women's Rural Institute or visiting relatives, her father put her to bed. She told him she could undress herself, but he liked to help. One night he had touched her. She thought it was an accident, but he did it again.

'I know what you would like,' he said.

She didn't say anything.

'And I'm going to get it for you. It's a secret. Don't tell Mammy.'

He touched her the next night her mother went to the Rural, then took her by the hand in her nightdress and Mickey Mouse floppy slippers out to the shed in the darkness. She was frightened until he snapped on the light. A red fairy cycle was leaning against his workbench, the present her mother had been promising her for the past few Christmases. She had never seen anything so beautiful, the way the handlebars gleamed and the spokes threw shadows on the shed floor. There was a label tied to the saddle, with her name and three crosses for kisses. He sat her on it in her nightdress and wheeled her about under the stars in the warm night. She wanted him to carry the cycle up the stairs to her bedroom.

'Mammy will make a row. I'll leave it in the porch, it'll be safe there.'

Mairi almost fell over the bicycle when she came back from the Rural with the baking she had won the prize for.

'That's spoiling her, Neil. It could have waited for her birthday, or you could have got her a second-hand one. There are adverts in the paper. Kids grow out of bikes quickly.'

'I sold the calf for a good price,' he said, shrugging his shoulders.

The bicycle had a bell and a basket on the front. Her father went up and down the road with her, holding on to the back of the saddle and the handlebars until she could keep her balance. The lapwings were tumbling from the sky as she rode up and down, ringing the bell for the pleasure of hearing the joyful tone while he ploughed the field on the old smoky Fordson. She leaned her bicycle carefully against the grassy verge so that she wouldn't chip the red paint, and laid the flowers she picked into the basket on the handlebars for her mother, who had started to teach her the Cave of Gold.

'Ead'rainn a' chruit, a' chruit, a' chruit. . .'

Between us the harp, the harp, the harp,
Between us the harp, my friends and I parted,
Between us her song, her song, her song. . .

Her father clapped, the cigarette in his mouth.

'Why are you standing like that?' her mother asked.

'I'm sore,' she said, looking at her father.

'Sore? Where?'

'You're embarrassing her, Mairi,' he said. 'It'll be the saddle; I'll adjust it.'

She stood looking at her feet, but couldn't get the words out.

She knew it was hopeless, her mother would never believe her. In the pain of her silence she saw his cigarette ash fall to the carpet and watched him scuffing it with his shoe.

'Off you go to bed now,' her mother ordered.

'I've got homework to do,' Cairistiona told her, going for her bag.

'But you don't get homework in primary,' her mother said. 'Why are you getting so difficult about going to bed? All this excitement about learning a song? How are you going to be when you're on the platform?'

'She'll be just fine,' her father said.

'I'll make you Horlicks so you'll sleep,' her mother offered.

She held the mug with the frothy white liquid in both hands, taking as long as possible to drink it, her father watching her, smiling.

'Time for bed,' her mother ordered, taking the mug from her. 'Daddy will come up and tuck you in.'

Though it was summer the bedroom was cold. She stood at the window in the coombed wall, looking across the machair to the mountains over the sound, wishing she were a bird. She would fly over to there and never come back, making a nest in a high cliff where nothing could reach her. She was shaking as she took off her clothes, pulling on the nightdress with the red bow at the neck, then slipping into bed, making herself into a tight little ball under the duvet when she heard his footsteps on the stairs. The door opened and closed, the bed moving as he stretched out beside her.

'You sing that song really well. You're going to get the medal, you know.'

She didn't answer.

When he put his hand under the clothes she thought of the Cave of Gold. As she learnt more of the song it was becoming a frightening place. The piper had been given a silver chanter so that he could play better than anyone, but after a year and a day he had to go down into the dark cave.

'Our secret,' her father said, smoothing back her hair. 'It's our secret. Aye, you're going to get the medal and I'm going to buy you a big bicycle with special things on it. That's our secret.' He said she could ride it to school, and he would get lights fitted for the dark nights. The next day she had a puncture on the road, a bent nail from a horseshoe from her grandfather's time. She was in tears as she looked at the deflated tyre, as if the bicycle were ruined, but he was coming over the field, holding down the barbed wire as he crossed the fence.

'We'll sort it,' he promised, squatting on his heels beside her and putting his arm round her shoulders. 'Away to the shed for my tool box.'

He removed the wheel and levered off the tyre, smeared adhesive on the gash in the tube, put a patch on it and rubbed the repair with blue chalk.

'We'll let it dry for a few minutes,' he explained before he screwed on the pump. 'Here, you do it.' He gripped the tyre as it got harder. 'There you are now, good as new. There aren't many things that can't be sorted.'

He went away, and she lay sobbing. She was frightened to go to sleep because she knew she would have a nightmare about the Cave of Gold. Her mother had told her the story that wasn't in the song. The piper's dog had come running out of the cave, mad-eyed and hairless, but there was no sign of the piper. An old woman at a well some distance from the cave could hear the sound of his pipes beneath her feet, a wail of despair from the darkness.

'What's happening to you, Cairistiona?' the teacher asked when she gave back the Gaelic test. 'You used to be top of the class, but now you're making silly mistakes. It's weeks since you got a gold star. And stop fidgeting in your seat as if you've got ants in your pants,' she added, making the other children laugh.

Her parents had spoken Gaelic to her even before they spoke English to her. She was the best in her class and knew more words than anyone else. They wanted her to be a teacher, but she didn't like Gaelic now.

'We'll try that verse again,' her mother told her after tea.

He was sitting watching her.

'I can't remember,' Cairistiona said.

'Can't remember, when we went over it three times last night?' her mother said, irritated. 'You're not paying attention. You're spending too much time on that bike. I'll tell you the words once and then you sing them.'

'Bidh na minn bheaga nan gobhair chreagach,
Mun tig mise, mun till mise a Uamh an Òir. . .'

The little kids will be goats of the crags
Before I arrive, before I return from the Cave of Gold. . .

'I'm going away to aunt Jessie's for the weekend,' her mother informed her. 'You can sing to Daddy.'

Cairistiona wanted to run after the car as her mother drove away, to tell her everything, but somehow she couldn't. She lay listening to the sound of the television set below, putting her fingers down her throat, trying to be sick. He came up as the cliffs across the sound were darkening, the roosting birds quiet.

'I'll lie here till you go to sleep.'

She didn't want to fall asleep in case he touched her, but her eyes were getting heavy. She was in the Cave of Gold, with arms around her in the darkness. Now a goat was pushing against her. When she woke she felt the pain inside her and beat her father away with her fists.

'I'll tell Mammy what you did!' she threatened, and when she saw the blood on the sheet she began to moan in terror.

'No, no,' he said, rocking her in his arms. 'It'll be all right.'

She found it difficult going down the stairs next morning because of the pain. She didn't make herself any food because she was feeling sick. She sat staring at the wall until she heard his pick-up, then the door opened and he wheeled in a red bicycle with gold bands. It had handlebars that swept down, many gears, and a dynamo.

'Try it,' he encouraged her. He wheeled it outside and held it for her while she put her feet into the straps on the pedals, but it was painful, sitting on the saddle. She rode it down the track, standing up on the pedals, and when she looked back she saw him watching her at the gable of the croft. It was fifteen miles to her auntie's, where Mammy was staying, but he would catch up with her in the pick-up and no one would believe her, because he had taken the sheet off her bed and put it into the washing machine.

If she took the bicycle he would keep on touching her. But it was beautiful and as she rode up the track to the house she moved the lever and felt the chain slackening and tightening again as the gears shifted. When she was about fifty yards from where he was waiting she twisted the handlebars violently and lay on the ground moaning by the spinning wheel as he came running, tossing away his cigarette.

'I hit a stone. It's my leg.'

He carried her upstairs, but when he tried to undress her she pretended to scream with the pain.

'I think you should get the doctor,' she sobbed.

'It'll be all right,' he soothed her. 'You've twisted your leg. I'll take the wheel into town to get it straightened.' He left her lying with her clothes on.

Mairi saw the new bicycle propped up against the wall when she drove up. She left the car door open and went to find him at his work-bench, filing something at the vice.

'This is the limit, Neil. Where did you get the money when I can't even get things for the house? The washing machine leaks every time I use it.'

'She deserves it, for the effort she's put into the song,' he said without turning round.

'Wouldn't it have been better waiting to see if she won the

medal before getting that for her? You're spoiling her, Neil. When she goes to the big school she'll come to expect things and she'll never be off our backs.'

'It's a few years yet before she goes away to the big school. Anyway, she's not that type of girl,' he added, the file rasping.

'I wish we'd had a son instead, because you wouldn't have spoilt him like this,' Mairi said heatedly. 'You'll change her and you'll regret it.'

Cairistiona heard the argument as she came round the corner.

'You're limping,' her mother said accusingly.

'I fell off the bike.'

'You could have broken your leg, after all that practice for the Mod. I hope you've been singing to Daddy while I was away.'

The night before the Mod they went over the song for the last time.

'Don't stand with your fingers locked like that; it's a sign that you're nervous, and the judges will notice,' her mother checked her.

Cairistiona took a breath as she'd been taught. Her mouth was open, but no words came.

'What's the matter?' her mother asked sharply.

'I can't remember the words.'

'Can't remember? We've gone over the song a dozen times, and you a native speaker. If this happens tomorrow who's going to help you?'

She ran out and went round the gable of the house by the peat stack. The cliffs across the sound were getting dark, and the birds would be settling for the night on their ledges where nothing could reach them, but she had no safe place to go to. She was losing everything, even the language she had been born with, the language her mother had sung her to sleep with, and there was no one to tell, not even in English.

She turned and saw the glow of his cigarette.

'You come back in and show Mammy you can do it,' he said, taking her hand. 'She wants you to get that medal and I'll buy you a gold chain for it.'

Next morning she locked the door before having a bath, and put a chair against the door handle as she buttoned the new white blouse with frills her mother bought her, buckling up the little kilt in her father's dark tartan.

The hall was full for the competition and she was the last of the six to sing.

'Is truagh mi rìgh gun trì lamhan. . .'

My sorrow that I don't have three hands,
Two for the pipes, two for the pipes,
My sorrow that I don't have three hands,
Two for the pipes, one for the sword.

The judges were sitting forward in their chairs, having put their marking pencils down. They had never heard the song performed with such emotion, and by someone so young. It was as if the girl on the platform was herself struggling in the darkness.

'Bidh na laoidh bheaga nan cro-eadraidh
Mu tig mise, mun till mise a Uamh an Òir. . .'

The little calves will be milking cows
Before I arrive, before I return from the Cave of Gold. . .

Her parents were sitting in the front row, her mother wearing the medal she had won for the same song. But Cairistiona was looking at her father, and he wasn't smiling any more.

' 'S iomadh maighdean òg fo cheud bhàrr
Theid a null, a theid a null. . .'

Many a young untouched maiden
Will cross over, will cross over,
Before I return from the Cave of Gold.

Suddenly Cairistiona felt the tightness around her chest slackening, and she was emerging into the light as she sang the chorus for the last time.

'Ead'rainn a luaidh, a luaidh, a luaidh. . .'

Between us her song, her song, her song. . .

As the applause continued her mother was on her feet, her arms out, but her father was sitting with his face in his hands, his shoulders shaking.

11
For the Fallen

On the day that the Territorials were mobilised, Charlie Mackenzie
had been down the island, with the lorry, delivering a new stove to
one of the big houses. One of the kitchen-maids had given him tea
and a scone and had suggested that they meet on her day off, and
by the time Charlie had made the necessary arrangements he was
late back on the road. The window of the lorry was down as he
drove along the hazardous stretch of road high above the sound a
mile or so from the town when he heard the sound of pipes and
drums. Immediately he put his boot down.

As the lorry came careering down the brae, people pressed
against the railings in terror. It roared along Main Street and as
Charlie hauled on the handbrake he leapt out and pushed his way
through the crowd on the pier, gathered to watch the Territorials
going off to war. There were already twelve feet between the steamer
and the pier, but Charlie held the ground record (twenty feet six
inches) for the long jump at the Games. As he landed on the deck

he went through the big drum.

He had joined the Territorial battalion of the Argyll and Sutherland Highlanders in 1936 because he was an expert shot, shattering all the clay pigeons at shoots, whatever the angle of trajectory. He reckoned that an army issue rifle would be useful in the poaching he did on the island estates, wandering the bens in winter, dressed in a thin jacket, dragging the carcass of the stag down through icy corries, and selling it to Neilly the butcher.

Charlie was also notorious for women and in those golden pre-war summers, locals at their open windows on Main Street watched the handsome blond young man sitting astride his motor cycle at the memorial clock while local lassies fought for the privilege of going on his pillion into the countryside. It was said that Charlie had had a passionate affair with one of the nannies from Colonel Ainsworthy's house across the bay and that she had had to return to France in a smock, whereas she had first stepped from the steamer in *culottes*.

He loved the Territorials because of the annual camp on the mainland every summer. For a fortnight he lived under canvas, taking part in exercises during the day and in the evening slipping out of camp to rendezvous with local women he had met in the cafés. He won medals for races and for wrestling, and when he came home, the fights to be his pillion passenger resumed. On the day he drove his lorry at reckless speed along Main Street, leaping on to the steamer, a maid at a high window of the Hebridean Hotel above the bay had had hysterics, because she had been promised that she was to be that evening's pillion passenger.

Charlie was sent to France with the Argylls, and was caught up in ferocious fighting in a château early in June, when the huge Dunkirk evacuation had been completed. For a week, seven of them held out against a force of two hundred Germans. Charlie had built a machine gun nest with books from the shelves, including first editions of Rousseau. But the Germans had driven a tank through the French windows, bringing down the well-endowed nymphs on the ceiling, so the defenders had retreated to another salon. There was no food in the kitchen, but someone had found a jar of pickled eggs. Bodies were piled up in the corridors to await burial, but rats got to them. Charlie had discovered the wine cellar, knocking the neck off a bottle of champagne from an exquisite year because he didn't know how to spring the cork with his thumbs. He took another four bottles upstairs for his comrades, since the pickled eggs had run out.

German reinforcements arrived to break down the walls with the barrels of tanks, since the doors were booby-trapped. The last his company saw of Charlie was of him standing on the staircase with a machine gun, blasting back the Germans. Before they were hustled away by their captors they heard the detonation of a grenade.

Charlie's mother was calm when she opened the War Office telegram, but when she conveyed the tragic news to her husband he cried like a child. She was a dignified woman and when she queued at the shops for her rations and people commiserated with her over her loss, she shrugged.

The town was used as a naval base and Alan Petrie, the fifteen year old apprentice of Munro the joiner, was helping to hammer together twenty coffins a week for the bodies washed ashore from torpedoed convoys. Mrs Mackenzie could not bear to part with her son's motor cycle, so she kept it in the shed, going out every Monday to dust the pillion on which so many shapely backsides had rested, the owners clasping Charlie round the waist as he roared off into the countryside for an evening of bliss in the bracken.

On VE night, Charlie Mackenzie's mother could hear the fire-works exploding above the bay, and into the wee small hours she heard the revellers lurching up the brae from the celebrations. A year later there was a ceremony at the war memorial which had been put up after the Great War and which featured a bronze soldier with backpack and rifle staring out to sea, as if expecting an invasion.

Having made a patriotic speech in which he claimed that the sacrifice had been necessary, Colonel Ainsworthy tugged a cord, and the union jack fluttered down, revealing a bronze plaque with the names of the dead in the second world conflict. There, in alphabetical order was: *Charles Mackenzie* MM

The Military Medal was a posthumous award because his comrades, released from their prison camp, testified to Charlie's fearless courage against hopeless odds in the château. But his mother didn't attend the unveiling ceremony at the war memorial, with a local child with a lisp reading the poem 'For the Fallen,' followed by the lone piper's lament going out over the sea. Instead Mrs Mackenzie tended her small vegetable patch, then went in to dust the motor cycle.

It was still a world of ration books, but the Mackenzies had killed one of their own hens for Christmas day, and on Christmas eve they went down the icy brae to the watchnight service in the church. As she sang the carols Mrs Mackenzie smiled, but her husband trembled beside her, thinking of these golden evenings by the clock, with his beloved son – the only one he had – sitting on his motor bike, hailing his father in Gaelic before roaring up the brae with his latest admirer on the pillion.

They were getting ready for bed when there was a knock on the door.

'Who is it, Calum?' his wife asked, coming through.

Their son was standing under the porch light.

'Why are you torturing us like this, when we've suffered so much?' the elderly man cried out in Gaelic in anguish. 'Why send our boy back as a *tannasg* (ghost) when he's lying dead in France in no known grave, as the letter said?'

But powerful arms were encircling him.

'I knew you would come back,' his mother said as her son lifted her off her feet.

'I'm a wee bit late, and I've brought someone back with me,'

Charlie told them, leading a figure by the hand into the light.

The last we saw of Private Charlie Mackenzie, with at least one bottle of *grand cru* champagne in him, was standing on the staircase of the wrecked château, kicking in the faces of Germans who were trying to get upstairs. The leading storm trooper drew the pin from a grenade with his teeth and lobbed it. Charlie had been the best footballer on the island, and before the grenade touched the stairs he had kicked it back. The explosion was heard by his fellow soldiers as they were being led away, and they assumed that Charlie had been killed.

But the grenade had blasted away the middle section of the staircase, taking most of the Germans with it, leaving Charlie standing at the top in mid-air. A bullet splintered the panelling beside him as he retreated into the château, racing along passages in his noisy boots, kicking open a door, rolling through the drapes of a four poster-bed, a scented negligee under the pillow. He saw through the big window his escape route over the roofs, and he used the butt of his gun on the glass.

Charlie was pursued among the maze of chimneys by two Germans. One of them was kneeling on the lead roof, taking careful aim, waiting for Charlie to appear, but he came up behind the German and slit his throat with his bayonet. The second soldier fired at the fugitive, but the bullet ricocheted, whining among the ornate chimneys. This German was kneeling to take aim again, but Charlie's boot struck him in the back and he went over the parapet, breaking his spine on a sundial.

Where does Charlie go from here? Clearly not down into the grounds, which are swarming with Germans. He remains on the roof, watching his platoon being led away, their hands above their heads, thinking that if he had a machine gun he could rescue them.

Charlie knows that other Germans will come up on to the roof to look for their comrades, so he makes for the back of the building where there is so far no sight of the enemy. It's a long way to the ground, but he has the pole vault record at the island Games and knows how to fall without injuring himself. Once on the ground he rolls among shrubbery and is gone.

But to where? He hasn't one word of French. How is he going to survive in an occupied country where the invaders are always on the look-out for soldiers on the run? It's approaching nightfall and Charlie is getting hungry. He goes up to the window of a sinister looking house set behind dark shrubberies and sees an old priest sitting at the end of a long mahogany table, helping himself from a tureen. Charlie watches the slices of lamb being laid on the blue plate, followed by a heap of Brussels sprouts. Charlie isn't a Catholic, but could easily become one to allow him to share the feast. As he watches the silver fork carrying the succulent food to the priest's mouth Charlie decides to make his move, rapping on the pane with his knuckles. The fork stops mid-way to the priest's mouth. He looks surprised, then alarmed when he sees the face at the glass, as if the devil has manifested in his parish. Charlie lifts the window and steps inside the room, pulling in his gun after him.

The *curé* is standing at the table, his hands up, but Charlie makes signs to show him that he means no harm. Instead he keeps pointing to his mouth. At first the priest thinks he's a dummy, but realises that this soldier is hungry, so he pushes the tureen towards Charlie, who helps himself to the lamb with his fingers. When he's wiped the inside of the dish clean with his fingers he starts on the vegetables.

He's stuffing the last of the sprouts into his mouth when the door opens and the priest's housekeeper comes in, carrying a tray with the stewed rhubarb which is so good for the priest's bowels. When she sees the intruder she drops the tray and faints. Charlie and the priest carry her through to another room. The priest indicates that he's going for a glass of water for her, and Charlie is slapping the housekeeper lightly on the cheeks when he hears the clicking sound.

The *curé* is making a phone call on the candlestick instrument.

Charlie can't be sure that he isn't calling the Germans, so he has no option but to rip the wires from the walls. He hates doing it, but he ties the priest to a chair, using the braided cord from the curtains.

Where does Charlie go, after having filled his pockets from the priest's cigarette box and emptied a decanter down his throat? He leaves the sinister house with its dripping shrubberies and wanders down a lane. There's an imposing stone gate, and he goes up the dark avenue. The château in front of him is even larger than the one he was defending. He prowls round the house, until he comes to a rectangle of light like a golden mat on the audible gravel.

A woman is playing a grand piano. There's a silver lamp reflected in the polished wood, the lithe figure of a woman lifting the yellow globe. At the side window Charlie watches the player's fingers flowing along the keys, noting the wedding ring and other sumptuous jewels. The tune takes him back to the island, to lying as a boy by a rippling stream. He leans against the wall and smokes one of the priest's cigarettes.

What is he going to do? The pianist has a sympathetic face, but will she welcome a fugitive Scottish soldier at this time of night? Perhaps her husband is elsewhere in the house, smoking a cigar in the library while reading a sporting journal, as Colonel Ainsworthy is known to do at home. What is the fugitive Highlander to do? Keep wandering, looking for a house where he'll get a bed? Doss down in an outhouse?

Charlie hasn't realised that the pianist has stopped playing, he's been so preoccupied with what to do. She has seen him, and has been studying him for the last minute or so, without leaving the piano stool. She can see his thoughtful profile in the lamplight as she watches the cigarette raised to his lips, the smoke slowly expelled as he deliberates. He has a strong appealing profile.

She felt no fear as she opened the French window and invited him to step inside. When he was a message boy with Black's, taking the basket across to the big house on the other side of the bay, he had been taught to bow to Mrs Ainsworthy before handing over the goods she had ordered. But was he to bow to this good-looking woman with the gold locket at her graceful throat who was smiling at him?

Then she spoke in English.

'Monsieur, where is your regiment?'

'Most of them have been taken away by the Germans.'

'Come and tell me your story,' she suggested, making a sign for him to follow her.

They went down a passage lined with oil paintings and she led him into an immense kitchen where an old woman was working at a long table like an executioner's block stained with the blood of past victims. The lady spoke in French to the cook, who eyed the soldier as she listened to her mistress's instructions. The cook slid a plate of veal and potatoes in front of him at the table, and though he had already had the priest's dinner, he set to this second helping, washed down with the carafe of wine that the woman brought to him.

'Now tell me your story,' she urged as she took a chair beside him.

'I came across some Germans and managed to get away.'

She shook her head. 'I want the whole story, the true story. Don't leave anything out. My husband is fighting against these bastards. And besides, I have read *Rob Roy* in English.'

So Charlie told her about the siege of the château, leaving out none of the details; neither the pickled eggs nor the pile of bodies in the salon, the family canvases mortally wounded by machine gun bullets, the kick he had given to the grenade on the stairs as they were coming up to get him.

'You're obviously a brave man,' she complimented him.

'Can I sleep in one of the outhouses?' he requested.

'Certainly not. A brave man who has helped to defend France will sleep in this house as an honoured guest. Will you make up a bed on the first floor, Suzanne?' she asked the aged servant.

'*Oui, Comtesse.*'

But first, would the brave Scottish soldier like a bath, after his exertions? The only bath in Charlie's house on the island was a zinc tub which his mother had filled in front of the fire and in which she had soaped his back. The bath the Countess showed him up to was the size of a rowing boat, and it filled in seconds from the gushing brass faucet. Charlie left his odorous uniform in a corner and stepped into the fragrant steam. He was closing his eyes, thinking of the Countess's figure when she came in with a long brush and proceeded to soap his back before scrubbing it gently.

Charlie was then given one of her absent husband's nightshirts and shown into a bedroom with a four-poster. He was settling to sleep when he heard the door open and the countess came in, shading a little night-light with her palm.

'You must be lonely,' she said, lying down beside him.

Charlie didn't move on from this billet. The Countess saw no sense in him trying to rejoin his unit, because the countryside was swarming with Germans, and Charlie was in no hurry to move on. As a lover the Countess was far in advance of any of the women he had had on the island, and with variations that would have shocked them, however free they were in other ways. Charlie worked outside in the grounds of the château, hacking back shrubbery to let more light in, and when a German patrol appeared he hid until they had gone away again. The Countess was worried that the Germans would loot the valuable works of art in the château, but Charlie promised to take care of them.

On the evening that the Countess learned that her husband had been killed, Charlie spent the night in a magnificent bed comforting her.

The woman at his elbow when he appeared at his parents' door after an absence of six years was wearing a fur coat and red leather boots up to her knees. Mrs Mackenzie was nervous about taking a grand lady into her humble home, but the visitor put the elderly woman at ease. Charlie described in Gaelic to his parents how he had survived, while the Countess sat smoking a cigarette of strong odour.

'I wrote to you several times to say that I was safe and well,' he told his parents, 'but of course I didn't put my address.'

'We never received your letters, son,' his father shook his head.

'I thought of trying to rejoin the Argylls, but then I heard on the wireless that they had been captured at St Valery and that most of them were prisoners. Then I thought, I must try to get back home, so Bridgette here arranged for me to be taken across the Pyrenees into Spain, but the guide was a traitor, and the Germans were waiting for me. I managed to break out two days before the war ended, but the Germans still had some ammunition to use up, the vindictive bastards, and I ended up with a dozen machine gun bullets in my body. I was in hospital till last month.'

'I knew you would come back,' his mother said, but didn't explain her certainty. 'Go and have a look at the war memorial.'

'We can do that tomorrow,' her son said.

'No, go up tonight, and take a torch so that you can read the names.'

Charlie and his lover in her coat of pelts down to her high-heeled boots walked up the brae arm in arm under the brilliant stars. Ahead was the silhouette of the soldier on the granite memorial. Charlie swept the beam of the torch up the new plaque that had been put up for the dead from the second war.

'God, I was in school with these people, and in the château with some of them.'

Then the beam stopped.

Charles Mackenzie MM

'Good God, they've put me on the memorial,' he told the Countess.

They hugged each other, their laughter ringing out over the dark sea where the bronze soldier gazed with his lifeless eyes, his useless gun by his side.

The next day the Countess gave the elderly couple their gifts. Mr Mackenzie got a bottle of French brandy, his wife a musical box on which a ballerina in a dainty muslin dress rotated to Strauss when the key on the base was wound up. The French visitor helped Mrs Mackenzie to prepare the Christmas dinner on the stove in the room that was also the living-room. The Countess had brought chestnuts from her forest, from which she made a stuffing. She had also brought a rich dark Christmas pudding made to a secret recipe by her old cook.

In the new year Charlie announced that they had to go back to France.

'But you're going to come with us,' he told them.

His parents looked at each and shook their heads.

'We were born here and we'll die here,' his mother said. Then she added in Gaelic: 'But you need to go, Charlie, with the great lady, because it will be a better life for you than hanging about Main Street on your motor bike, which can be sold now.'

Charlie and the Countess went away on the morning steamer. He was to die in France, aged seventy two, in the bed of the Countess, whose nightdress – by Coco Chanel – lay on the floor during the last blissful hours of his life. Nobody got round to erasing his name from the war memorial, though he came home many times to see his aged parents.

12
Celtic Roots

Dr Mary Fielding lived in a world of patients and horses. She was a general practitioner in Somerset and on the family farm she kept six horses. In the early morning before she set out for her practice in Glastonbury she would jump a horse over the black and white posts set up on the pasture, the breaths of rider and mount mingling in the morning air.

She loved the area's association with King Arthur, and after evening surgery would climb up to the Tor, to sit looking over the Somerset Levels. She felt that she had some kind of healing gift, because some of her patients had told her that they had felt a 'warm glow' during consultations, and that her presence was more effective than a prescription.

She was a good-looking woman, tall, fair haired, physically attractive as she bobbed along on a horse. She had had several affairs, all unsatisfactory, and devoted all of her time to her patients and her horses. She thought nothing of turning out of her bed in the middle of the night to answer a call, even if it were only stomach cramps.

Then, one August, she got a new patient, Andrew Shipton, a builder whose hobby was breeding Dobermann dogs. A magnificent sleek specimen lay at his feet as he told his new doctor about the reason for his first visit to her surgery.

'I've done something to my shoulder.'

When he took off his shirt and she requested him to raise his arms she saw the ripples of his muscles.

'Where is the pain?' she asked, pressing.

'There.'

'You've pulled a muscle. Were you lifting something heavier than usual?'

'No, I was dowsing.'

'Dowsing?'

'Yes. I was looking for water in a field. I was walking about with a forked stick when it jerked suddenly, so violently.'

'And was there water there?' she asked, sitting down in wonder.

'There was. One of the men dug for it. It's a lovely pure underground stream.'

'When did you discover that you had this gift?' she wanted to know.

'It's in the family. We come from Cornwall.'

'Celts,' she said with admiration. 'I have Celtic blood in me too.' She was scribbling a prescription as she spoke. 'These are painkillers. They'll help till the muscle begins to heal itself.' She was now writing on a piece of paper. 'This is my address. I've been trying for ages to find if there's water in a field for my horses. I'm having to carry buckets over two fields. Would you be able to come round when your shoulder's better?'

He was at her family's farm the following week, sitting beside her in the Land Rover as they bounced along the rutted track.

'How long have you kept horses?' he enquired.

'There's a joke in my family that I was born in the saddle.'

'They're fine animals,' he enthused as the six of them came trotting towards the fence, their manes lifting in the breeze.

He had brought with him a forked stick and he began to walk systematically round the field with it gripped between both his hands, as if he were steering a plough behind horses. She sat on the gate, fondling a horse's head on either side of her as she watched him. He looked like part of the landscape, like the steeple in the distance, except that he was alive, animated, a strong Celtic man with a gift in his hands.

As the stick began to jerk violently he called her over.

'Bring the spade from the back of the vehicle.'

After ten minutes of digging water was welling round his boots.

'I don't believe it,' she said.

'If you get someone to build a concrete trough your horses can drink here till their hearts' content.'

She took him into the house to meet her mother, the wife of a gentleman farmer who had never got her hands dirty on the property in her life. Her husband was dead and she had a manager to run the place.

'I was always sceptical about dowsing, but you've proved that it works,' Mrs Fielding said, giving the visitor a generous whisky. 'It makes it so much easier for Mary, with the horses, and her busy practice.'

'I was wondering, would you be able to make me the concrete trough?' Dr Fielding asked. 'I'll pay you, of course.'

Andrew knew that she was attracted to him, and that it was her way of getting him back on the farm without her mother becoming suspicious. He was in the field every night for a week, with his Dobermanns for company, digging out the soil, then hammering together the shutter for the concrete he poured from the mixer she had towed into the field for him.

They stood together, watching the horses drinking at the new trough.

'It makes such a difference,' she told him. 'I'll be able to stay in bed an extra half hour. There's something else I'd like your advice about.'

She drove him through four gates to a building on the edge of the farm, hidden in a dip.

'This is the old shearing shed,' she informed him. 'It fell into disrepair when we stopped keeping so many sheep and went more into cattle instead. I'd like to do it up, to use it as a place I could retreat to – you know the kind of thing, with a chair and a table, so that I could read and doze in summer when I've got some time to myself.'

Every evening after surgery she crossed the field to see how his repairs were progressing.

'It's nearly finished,' he told her as he hammered on a new board.

She didn't want him to leave, but knew that she didn't have another task for him.

'I'll be back Saturday afternoon to put the new door on,' he told her. 'Then you can sit out here till your heart's content.'

The housekeeper was off on the Saturday, and Mary put together a picnic in the kitchen and took it in a basket to the new hut. He asked her to hold the door while he put the screws into the last hinge.

'It's in a nice situation,' he said as he stood beside her at the new window with its view across fields to the Tor.

Andrew helped her to carry in the folding table and two chairs from her Land Rover, and set them up while she unpacked the basket, putting the wine bottle between the padded knees of her jodhpurs to draw the cork.

'To your hideaway,' he said, clinking his glass against hers.

'Tell me about your job, Andrew,' she asked as she passed him a sandwich which he shared with the Dobermann sprawled at his boots.

'I used to be a civil servant.'

'I don't believe you.'

'It's true. I used to sit at a desk in the Ministry of Defence in London, working on weapons allocations. Then one afternoon I said to myself: what the hell am I doing this for, when I could be outside? So I took my jacket off its hook, emptied my desk into the wastepaper basket and came down to Somerset because I've always been fascinated by the Arthurian legend. I wanted to work with my hands, you see, because as a boy I'd been good at fixing and making things.'

'And you've been doing this ever since?' she said in admiration.

'There's plenty of building work going about, and I'm also a dowser.'

'How did you get into that?' she wanted to know.

'My grandfather had the gift. He used to dowse for water in Cornwall.'

She managed to prolong the lunch for an hour, after all the food had been eaten, the wine drunk.

Andrew came to see her three times a week, with his own key for the shed. She had brought across a curtain, and they undressed by the light of a tiny torch because she was frightened the glimmer could be seen from the house. They lay on a mattress she had dragged from one of the unused bedrooms in the house, telling her mother that she was taking it to the dump because it was damp.

'Are we expecting visitors when you're moving beds?' her mother asked.

One night they drove into Glastonbury and ascended the Tor, lying down on the summit in the moonlight.

'Don't you feel the vibrations?' he asked as his body shielded hers from the wind.

It felt as if she were rising out of her body and circling round the Arthurian site.

She found that she couldn't get enough sex, like a horse that has so much energy, it wants to keep galloping. When she came she shouted out 'Oh *no*!' as if the sensation were too much for her, and then she rested on the mattress on the floor of the shed.

'I could sleep here all night with you,' she murmured. 'We wouldn't get up for work in the morning. First thing I would put you inside me. Andrew, I need you to spend more time with me.'

'My wife will get suspicious,' he warned her.

He had already told her that he was married, with two teenage children.

'I want you to leave her,' she said abruptly.

'Leave her?' he asked, confused. 'Where would I go?'

She walked naked across the shed to pick up her handbag from the corner.

'What do you think of this?' she asked, spreading it out on the chest of drawers he had treated for woodworm.

It was a page of advertisements torn from a farming paper, showing properties for sale. The one she had circled was a thousand acre hill farm on an island in the Hebrides.

'I've never heard of the place,' he said, studying the schedule.

'I've looked it up in an atlas. It's under an hour from the mainland by car ferry.'

'Why would you give up your medical practice?' he asked cautiously.

'I've always wanted to be a full-time farmer. It was my mother who pushed me into medicine, so that she could boast that she had a daughter who was a doctor, not dirtying her hands in the mire.'

'It's two hundred thousand pounds,' he pointed out. 'How would you finance it?'

'I've got my inheritance from father. I wouldn't give up medicine entirely, though. I could do locums for the doctor on the island, when he wanted to go away on holiday.'

'You've got it all thought out,' he said. 'Have you put in a bid?'

'I wouldn't do that without discussing it with you.'

'What's it got to do with me?'

'Because you have to come too, as my partner and my lover,'

she told him, stretching out her hand to him. 'That's why I want to move away from here, so that we can be together.'

'I've got my wife and the kids,' he reminded her.

'Yes, but you're not in love with her; you told me that. We're both Celts, Andrew: we've got the love and the experience to make this place work. It would be a new life for both of us, a fulfilling one. I won't have any objection to you supporting your wife and children out of the profits. Well, what do you say? I was speaking with the agent on the phone yesterday and he said that several other people are interested in the farm, so we would have to move on it.'

'They always say that,' her lover cautioned her.

Six months later Dr Fielding's horses came off the ferry in six red boxes, and were towed along the single track road in the Land Rover driven by her lover, who had left his family for the seductive Hebrides. In the back of the vehicle were his two Dobermanns which he hadn't been able to leave behind.

'I have a surprise for you,' she told him, taking his hand outside after she had shown him the house. They crossed a fence in the direction of the shore.

'We've got a standing stone!' she shouted, running up the hill in front of him and wrapping her arms around the inclined pillar protruding from the heather. 'I can feel the energies, just like the Tor at Glastonbury. This place is going to work for us, my love.'

Two days later Dr Mary was in the office of Archie Maclean, the island banker. His newest client was one of his most attractive, in his estimation.

'Farming has never been easy on this island,' he cautioned her as he stood at his usual stance, looking out of his window, along Main Street. 'The ground is poor, and if the ferry can't sail because of the weather, and the farmers can't get their beasts off the island to the sales, they lose a lot of money.

'But you're different, doctor,' he said, turning from the window to admire her again. 'You don't come here with the romantic dream of making a living from farming. You're bred to farming, so to speak. Besides which, you have no mortgage on the farm which I see you paid two hundred and ten thousand to Scrymgeour for. In my opinion you could have negotiated a better price, but you were using mainland solicitors who wouldn't understand the ways of doing business on this island. A photograph in an advertisement always looks better than the real thing.'

'But I do need to borrow,' the attractive customer said. 'I've used up all my capital buying the farm, and I need to stock it and make improvements.'

'How much do you require?' he asked.

'Twenty thousand?' she said, producing the sheet of paper she had done her sums on.

'I think I can persuade Head Office to advance you that,' the banker said, 'especially when they'll have the title deeds of the farm as security. Are you intending to work this place alone?'

'I've got a partner.'

The banker waited for a more detailed definition of this word, but none was forthcoming.

'And does your partner have farming experience?' he asked.

'Not exactly, but he's good with his hands.'

'That's important on this island,' the banker conceded.

The attractive doctor went away to feed her half dozen horses, which were now in the pasture by the sea. There were repairs needed to the farmhouse that Dr Fielding had missed on her inspection visit, because the seller went round with her, doing so much talking that she was distracted. Her lover was in their bedroom, probing the sodden plaster and explaining that he would have to go up on to the roof to replace slates.

But she loved the farm. She loved waking up under the coombed ceilings in the dawn and turning to him receptively before she went downstairs to fry the eggs and bacon on the old dependable Aga. She loved tramping across the acidic soil to feed the horses, which had spent the night in the stone shelter that looked like an ancient monument.

Her lover seemed to thrive in the salt-laden atmosphere, turning the handle to kick-start the grey Fordson that was now so old, spares were difficult to obtain. He had brought his shotguns with him and came in one evening, with a young deer draped round his neck, gralloching it at the back door and throwing the guts to the two dogs.

When she drove into town the doctor always paid a visit to the bank manager because she liked his old-world courtesy and valued his shrewd knowledge of island life.

'I'm delighted to hear you're doing so well on the farm, Mary,' the banker began. 'It shows what hard work can achieve, a commodity that is sadly scarce on this island where everything is put off until tomorrow and of course, tomorrow never comes. And your partner is well?'

'Very well.'

The bank manager had seen him alighting from the Land Rover on Main Street, the two Dobermanns slinking after him. Even at a distance Archie Maclean didn't like the look of the man. There was, he felt, a hidden violence there, though there were no signs of assault on this gentle woman's face as she sat opposite him, asking him about the possibility of becoming the local doctor's locum.

'Dr Murdoch never goes on holiday, much to the sadness of his patients,' the banker explained. 'If he did go, the mortality rate on the island would be lower.'

'Should I go to see him?' Dr Fielding asked.

'By all means. But be prepared for a long lecture on fairies. The doctor is more interested in the little people who live under the mounds on the Ross than in his patients. Some people think he holds a surgery down there, for whatever ailments fairies suffer from.'

But six months later, Dr Murdoch announced that he was going to retire at the age of seventy, to write a book, long in preparation, about the little people of the island. A new doctor came from the mainland and he was happy to use Dr Fielding as his locum, offering her two surgeries a week initially.

She was a very popular doctor, especially among the men. Males with very little wrong with them made appointments for the pleasure of admiring the fair-haired, big-busted physician across the desk who was happy to write prescriptions for them, but who stopped short of physical examinations she considered to be unnecessary.

She found the time to join the Farmers' Union on the island and to sit on the committee that ran the annual agricultural show. They respected her because she wasn't afraid to get her hands dirty and because she had been raised on a farm and knew about the problems as well as the pleasures.

While she was away doing surgeries or sitting on committees, Andrew was running the farm. He was up at first light and sometimes didn't get to bed until after midnight. One Spring evening, when he was ploughing by the light of the huge moon, she had crossed the furrows in her nightdress and dragged him from the tractor to make love to her against the standing stone above the sound. She believed that a ley line ran from the standing stone on their farm to the Tor above Glastonbury and that energy was being transmitted from there.

But even though he was a Celt too, Andrew didn't feel the reviving force of the ley line as he took her against the standing stone, with his two dogs lying nearby, as if they were the guardians of the ancient site. He wanted to get back down to his tractor so that he could finish the ploughing before the bad weather moved in from the Atlantic.

He found decay instead of regeneration, sheep stinking to high heaven in the bottom of gullies by the sea. One evening he had to drive a tractor across a bog, chains round the neck of the cow in order to save it from being submerged. In the mornings when his partner turned towards him he made an excuse and left the bed.

He was morose at table and complained when a surgery ran late.

'But I can't turn away the people and the money's so useful,' she told him. 'Jim has asked me to take his surgeries next week because he's going to the mainland for his daughter's wedding.'

'Tell him that he can't go,' her lover ordered her.

'I can't do that,' she said, shocked. 'It's a big day.'

'You'll be in town all day, what with the surgeries and calls to make and I'll be left here with everything.'

'I'm sorry, Andrew, but I think you're being unreasonable.'

'Fuck you,' he said, slamming the door as he went out.

She went to the window and stood looking down the slope to the horses by the sea. There wasn't even time to ride them now. He was right: she had come to the island as a farmer, but was turning into a doctor again. She hadn't told him that Jim was talking about a partnership, if the Health Board would finance a second doctor on the island, a necessity in the summer with the increasing number of visitors brought by the car ferry that ran constantly seven days a week.

At the beginning he had loved the island, rising to stand at the window and look out at the sun rising over the sound, sparkling on the granite pillar of the standing stone that seemed to ignite the day for him. He loved the colours of autumn, the golden leaves whispering round his wellingtons as he crossed the yard to couple the soporific cows to the rubber suctions on the milking machine they had installed. He loved sharing a bed with Mary, because she was an eager, passionate woman in contrast to his cold wife.

But the greyness of winter depressed him. The lichened dykes seemed to converge, hemming him in as he walked across the sodden field, his wellingtons weighed down with mud. He hated the still greyness of the sea, the cry of the buzzard, the lack of light, as if he were living in a nether-world. He had tried to dowse for water, to find a spring for the horses, but the forked stick shook with cold, not inspiration, between his chilled hands.

Then the winter gales began, as if the bedroom window were being wrenched out. It made him nervous and clumsy, making love to Mary. He hated the havoc that the gales caused, the branches of trees strewn around the house, the slates shattered on the ground.

There was something else he hated: the sound of Gaelic. She was learning the language using tapes, and some nights, when he wanted her badly, she wouldn't come upstairs. He lay in bed, hearing her repeating the same word over and over until he could have wrecked the room in his frustration.

'Why do you want to learn Gaelic?' he asked aggressively when she came up at last.

'Because I want to be able to speak it.'

'But there's hardly anyone who speaks it on the island.'

'Archie Maclean uses it all the time in the bank. And some of my elderly patients speak it. I would like to be able to speak with them.'

'But you're only a locum – you hardly see them,' he pointed out. 'Why waste your time? There are other things you could be doing.'

'Such as?' she asked as she lifted her sweater above her head.

'We could redecorate the house. It hasn't been touched in years.'

'But I like it the way it is.'

He could have said: *but that wasn't the way your mother's house was. Everything had to be just so. She had in these expensive decorators, with rolls of wallpaper that cost a fortune.* Instead he turned away from her as she entered the bed, his passion replaced by anger.

Their relationship was deteriorating and they were shouting at each other. This evening she was late home from the surgery because she had had to stitch a wound. She expected her partner to have a meal on the Aga, but instead he was sitting by the fire. She was tired and on edge, but decided not to say anything, so she put the pan on the hot plate and fried two steaks. She had to call him twice to the table, and he spat out the first mouthful.

'It's overdone. You know I like it with the blood running.'

'I'm sorry, I forgot. I've had a busy surgery.'

'I want you to give it up.'

'But I can't give it up. We need the money. We've got to pay your wife's alimony out of it.'

'So you're saying it's my fault that you've got to work at the surgery,' he challenged her.

'I'm not saying that at all. We made the arrangement before I bought this place.'

The light above him seemed to explode into his head. He picked up his plate and threw it across the kitchen where it shattered against the wall, the steak slowly sliding down, leaving a red slime.

'You wasteful bastard!' she shouted at him. 'I paid for that meat, and this is my house.'

When he had first met her in Somerset she had looked so desirable in her jodhpurs, with her fair hair held in a ribbon, and she had been so friendly. Now he saw how she had let herself go since coming to the island. She had taken the surgery in a sweater and denims, and there was dirt under her fingernails.

'I've put a lot of work into this place,' he defended himself. 'Getting up in the dawn to feed the cattle, ploughing the fields.'

'What else would you do?' she challenged him. 'Sit here doing nothing on my money?'

'Fuck your money.'

As she stepped forward to slap his face one of the dogs rose snarling in the corner. She kicked it aside as she wrestled with the door handle, her shoes clattering down the stone corridor, fumbling for the bolt in the darkness. As she stumbled across the quagmire of the yard towards the Land Rover she heard the two Dobermanns coming after her. He had told her that in eastern countries they were used to hunt down criminals.

'Call them off!' she shrieked.

But one of them had her by the ankle as she clambered into

the vehicle. She struggled but it wouldn't let go, and in desperation she groped in the dashboard, found a tool and brought it down on the dog's skull.

'You've killed it!' he shouted. Then, to the other dog: 'get her!'

Her savaged ankle was agony as she pushed down on the clutch, trying to start the vehicle, but he had pulled open the door to let the dog in. When she saw it rearing snarling, turned into a demon by his commands, she reached behind, grasped her medical bag and smashed it against the dog's head.

He was holding on to the handle, slithering across the mud as she turned the Land Rover towards the main road, but when she swerved towards the wall he had to let go, otherwise he would be crushed.

The vehicle stalled on the hill because she had forgotten to get petrol. He was coming running up after her, but the car approaching from the opposite direction dazzled him.

When the police came looking for him he was kneeling sobbing in the mud of the yard, cradling the corpse of one of his Dobermanns in his arms. He had to shoot the other one. He asked them to let him bury the dogs before they took him in, and they acceded to the request, otherwise someone else would have to dispose of the brutes. Next morning he was taken to the mainland on the steamer, handcuffed, with a coat over his head, though everyone knew who it was and what he had done.

A week later Mary went to see the bank manager, laying her crutches across his desk.

'You came very near to being killed,' he said as she described the attack.

'I've got twelve stitches in my calf,' she told him. 'The dog bit me through to the bone.'

He didn't ask her why their relationship had gone wrong because he had known other amorous couples who had come to the island and had ended their affair in violence and recrimination.

Archie Maclean had speculated before that it must be something in the air of the island that attracted these highly-sexed incomers.

'Will you sell the farm?' he enquired.

'Why should I do that?' she said, taken aback.

'Because of the ghastly memories.'

'Oh no, I'm going to stay here. I love this island and it's my home now.'

'But you won't be able to run the farm alone,' he pointed out.

'I'll advertise for a man – but not one with dogs.'

13
Laying To Rest

Dr Aonghas Macdonald came home on the last ferry, in a coffin.
His feet were pointing to the ramp, and for the hour-long crossing
his remains lay beside a refrigerated lorry. The seamen talked in
Gaelic about the doctor, who was known throughout the islands.
He had been a good piper, and on his instructions his ivory and
silver pipes were in the coffin with him. When the ramp went down
they carried him off on their shoulders to the hearse that had backed
down the pier.

Morrison the undertaker had received his instructions by fax
from the doctor's lawyers in Edinburgh because there were no
known relatives. The doctor, who was seventy nine, had never
married. He had been a quiet studious man who had written an
important paper on an infectious disease. He had also been a keen
lepidopterist, going about the island with a butterfly net and a torch
as a youth, discovering a new type of moth which had been given
his name.

No flowers had come with the coffin, which was driven the twenty five miles along the coastal road to the town, the driver having to stop often to let sheep cross. The coffin was carried into the parish church above the bay in which the doctor had been christened and in which his parents had been married. He was the son of the local schoolmaster and an island woman who had been a great Gaelic singer, and his own Gaelic had been impeccable. A black bordered card among assorted tools in Black's window on Main Street intimated that there would be a short service up in the parish church before interment.

Two women came off the ferry that evening. They were travelling separately, and the driver put their cases in the boot of the bus waiting on the pier. They paid their fares – return tickets – and sat in different parts of the bus.

'Where do you want dropped off, ladies'? the driver asked.

'The Hebridean Hotel,' both said.

Though it wasn't on his route he took the bus up the steep hill to the hotel above the bay. The two women had rooms with private bathrooms, with views of the bay. They sat at separate tables in the dining-room, each with a little candle glowing in a glass container, eating seafood from the à la carte menu. One had prawns, breaking them up in her fingers; the other forked the meat from lobster claws. One had a glass of Spanish wine; the other sipped mineral water with ice and lemon.

They went into the lounge for coffee, sitting with their individual silver pots and little dishes of *petits fours* on doilies. They were both beautiful and dressed at the height of fashion, with rings on their fingers, lacquer on their nails. One had a Celtic cross at her throat. At the desk they both ordered a call for eight o'clock the next morning. Both slept soundly, their windows open on the bay.

The church wasn't full for the service because Dr Macdonald had been away for so long that a generation didn't know him. The two women walked up the brae. One was dressed in a black costume, with a pillbox hat from which a veil hung. The other was wearing a dress patterned with flowers, and a wide-brimmed straw hat. Their heels were high.

They entered the cool vestry of the church, each taking a hymn book in a gloved hand from the beadle, and sat in different pews near the front, where the doctor's coffin rested on trestles. The minister called for *Abide with Me*. One woman was a mezzo-soprano, the other a contralto, and their combined voices went out through the vestry and across the bay where a man cutting bracken heard them and sat down to listen. When the minister asked the mourners to join him in prayer the two women put their gloved hands together and closed their eyes.

'We remember Dr Aonghas,' the minister said. 'We remember his love of learning, his devotion to his profession, the purity of his Gaelic.'

The coffin was carried out of the church to the heavy tread of the organ. The two women joined the other mourners, walking behind the slow hearse up the hill, past the ruined smithy where the dead man's people had plunged the hissing iron into the trough of water while hooves from all over the island waited to be shod.

A local man closed the gate of the cemetery behind him and turned to the two women.

'You can't come in here, ladies.'

The woman in the floral dress arched an eyebrow. The other one lifted her veil with spread fingers.

'Women don't go to funerals in these parts,' he explained.

But the one in black pushed open the gate, and the other woman followed her up the gravel path to the doctor's family lair which had been opened. Dr Macdonald had no close friends left in the community, but the undertaker had phoned around to find eight names to put on the cards for the allocation of cords. He had the cards in his hand, calling out the head cord first. A notable piper came forward to take it, but the woman in black was already by the undertaker's side and her glove plucked the card from his hand. The undertaker looked uneasy, but called out the cord for the feet. He was about to read the name but the other woman stepped forward and took the card.

The minister went up to the two women and put an arm round each. He spoke to them, and they whispered to him, their lips close to his ears. He nodded, then opened his Bible to read a prayer.

The woman in black took the strain of the head cord, the other woman the feet cord, the heels of their elegant shoes sinking into the heaped soil. The three men on either side took the strain as Dr Aonghas Macdonald was lowered into his grave. When the coffin was on the bottom both women threw in a handful of earth.

The deceased's lawyers had authorised the expenditure of £200 in the Arms for whisky and sandwiches for the mourners. Both women drank whisky neat, but when locals tried to make conversation they turned away to the windows, to gaze out over the bay as if they were expecting a boat to come in.

'I've never seen a woman at a graveside in my life before,' an old timer complained to the minister. 'And I've certainly never seen one, far less two, getting a cord. Why did you give them the cords?'

'They have come a long way,' was all the minister would say.

The two women went back on the afternoon bus with their boat tickets in their gloves. But this time they sat together, talking, pointing out seals on a rock, a yacht tacking up the sound. On the ferry they ate a meal together, and afterwards went into the bar where there was much laughter.

It was said on the island that one of the women was Dr Aonghas's common-law wife, and that the other was her sister. Other stories went round in Gaelic, and it appeared that the doctor had collected more than moths.

14
Dispossessed

The croft at the top of the town had been in the MacKinnon family for longer than anyone could remember, certainly over a hundred years, because in 1883, at the time when the Napier Commission arrived to hear the crofters' grievances, Uisdean MacKinnon was one of those who gave evidence.

He was a big handsome fellow, his bushy beard making him look even more impressive as he stood in front of the visiting delegation in his working clothes, the mud of his croft still on his boots, his cap tucked into the leather belt at his waist. Most of the witnesses were giving their testimonies in Gaelic, but though Uisdean was effortlessly fluent in his native tongue, he had decided to give his observations in English, because he spoke quickly and eloquently, and knew that the interpreter wouldn't have the time or the skills to translate the full force of his words for the benefit of the Commissioners, worthy impartial men who sat in the courthouse, their top hats under their chairs. At last the common voice was to be heard.

Uisdean MacKinnon began by explaining that he and his family were the tenants of a two acre croft at the top of the town. Did the witness have clear titles to the land? one of the Commissioners interrupted Uisdean's introduction. No, but it had always been understood, and honoured, that his family were the tenants, and they had duly paid the rent on time to the factor.

Was the rent fair? another Commissioner enquired.

But Uisdean would not be hurried. He wanted to establish that he had the authority to testify about the history of the town, since his family had been there for generations, so the Commissioners settled back in the sunlight coming in the long window to listen to this eloquent history lesson.

He explained that the town was divided between two separate estates, a MacLean laird who had been there for centuries, but who had had to sell the other half in the early nineteenth century because of gambling debts. A legal family from Edinburgh, the Finlaysons, were the purchasers, and the MacKinnon croft at the top of the town was on Finlayson land.

Uisdean went on to describe how, in 1846, his father had dug up the potato patch on their croft, splitting the first of the crop with his knife to lay bare the black heart. The blight had arrived from Ireland, borne by the wind or by the boots of a visitor. The potato failed throughout the island and elsewhere, and within six months the population of the town had doubled to over a thousand as starving people trekked in from the rest of the island in search of food. The cargo of meal sent by the Poor Relief had provoked disturbances when it was unloaded from the vessel. One man had slashed one of the sacks with a knife and held his hat under the spillage. When the meal came to be distributed in the area where the memorial clock now stands, police from the mainland were present with drawn truncheons, and when the last sack was shaken upside down for the last few flakes there were still hundreds of starving people, including many children.

'There wasn't enough timber to make coffins,' Uisdean testified to the sombre Commissioners. 'I can remember going along the shore with my father, looking for flotsam, to see if we could salvage sufficient boards to make a coffin for my sister Iseabail, who died at the age of nine, with her stomach swollen, like a cow's with colic. And there wasn't sufficient room in the cemetery, so we buried my sister in a corner of our croft, God rest her soul, and from that day on we have never put plough or spade near that spot.'

One evening a brig had come into the bay, anchoring a hundred yards offshore, in the vicinity of the site where the Spanish Armada galleon, allegedly laden with gold to pay the invasion force, had been blown up by the treacherous MacLeans. Word went round that there were two hundred sacks of meal in the hold of the new arrival. The people congregated on the seafront, which at that time had no railings, and in the press one man was pushed into the water and drowned, too weak with hunger, and too depressed to swim.

But the vessel had come to pick up a cargo, not to discharge one. Major Finlayson had chartered the brig, having decided that the only way to reduce the population was by emigration.

'The laird was claiming that he had the best interests of the island folk at heart,' Uisdean MacKinnon observed. 'But in reality he was clearing his estate to make way for sheep, which he evidently thought were more profitable and less trouble than humans.'

'How many went on that emigrant ship?' one of the Commissioners, who had been making notes, asked.

'It depends what you meant by "went", sir,' Uisdean answered. 'I take the verb to mean going of one's own accord. Bear with me, gentlemen, while I take some time to answer your question. Most of the people didn't want to leave, but Matheson the minister preached a sermon in Gaelic in the open air in which he said that it was wicked to resist the attempts of Major Finlayson to provide a better life for us on the other side of the ocean. He described a land with tall straight pines that could be felled to make homesteads, and fertile ground that could be planted with wheat. I can remember his very words that day, and I'll translate them into English to give you the gist of what he told us in Gaelic, of which he was a great scholar: "In two years' time you will be sitting by your blazing fires in your comfortable new homes, with ample food in the cupboard, and your healthy children sleeping peacefully in their cots. This island will be a bad memory." '

Uisdean MacKinnon paused for effect in the dead silence of the old courtroom, where it seemed that the row of Commissioners had stopped breathing.

'Two hundred people went on that emigrant brig after the Reverend Matheson's sermon, but there were still spaces for another hundred. My own family refused to go, though the factor came round to say that we had to go on board immediately, because every day that the ship lay in the bay was costing the Major money.'

Two days later six horses were led down the gangway of the steamer from Glasgow by their riders, burly men in hacking jackets and breeches, with coiled horsewhips. On Major Finlayson's instructions the factor had hired them in order to round up the stragglers who were refusing to go on the vessel in the bay.

'I was a boy of ten at the time,' Uisdean began his vivid reconstruction of the scene. 'It was said that they had been persuaded with plenty of grog and the promise of five guineas each to come to the island to do the laird's bidding. They were brutal looking men with spurs and whips. I saw them riding up the hill in a line in the early morning, against the backdrop of the bay, with the ship below, waiting to sail. The horses jumped the wall and came trotting across our croft, ruining the crops we had recently planted.

'The horsemen warned my father that we had to get down to the harbour within the hour, but he pretended that he only spoke Gaelic and couldn't understand them. They leapt the wall again and went on to the next croft with the same message, but were back with us within the hour.'

This time one of them was carrying a firebrand in his fist. Though the MacKinnon family – six children – were huddled in the house, the riders hacked at the flanks of their mounts with their spurs, backing them against the mortarless stonework and bringing it down, in the course of which one of the children sustained a broken leg. The roof was ablaze on the ground.

'My sisters were screaming and our mother was shouting that we had to get down to the boat as soon as possible, but my father said: "No, we're not going. Killing us on our own soil will be preferable to sailing to a strange country in that hulk down there. The minister made out that Canada is a land of milk and honey, but I've heard old sailors talk about it, and it's a place of grizzly bears and Indians with poisoned arrows.'

'So you didn't embark?' one of the Commissioners asked Uisdean.

'We didn't. We hid in the woods above the bay and watched the people being put aboard by the hired men who'd tied their horses to the pump outside the Free Church. We were a mile away but we could hear the screaming. I have good eyesight, and I saw one old woman being lifted by the waist and actually dropped into one of the boats that was ferrying the people out to the brig. There was a big trunk in the bow of one of the boats, and someone stood up, with their arms raised, screaming that they would never see this dear place again, when the trunk shifted, capsizing the boat, drowning the eight souls.

'My family saw scenes that day that continue to give those of us who are left nightmares, and there are summer evenings when I am scything when I suddenly hear the screams rising from the bay, and I know that the dead have not settled in the place where the Good Book says they go to for eternal rest.'

'What happened to your family, Mr MacKinnon?' another Commissioner, much moved, asked.

'The emigrant brig sailed at sunset that day. We watched it going out of the bay, but dared not light a fire to warm and feed ourselves, because the laird's hired horsemen were searching for us. We lay up in the woods for a week, existing on shellfish I picked from the shore of a secluded bay until the horses were led back onto the Glasgow steamer, and then we went home.'

'Home.' He laughed bitterly. 'The turf roof had been burned, and the rafters were blackened, the stones scattered. "We are going to rebuild this place," my father vowed. My mother pointed out that the factor would have it pulled down again, but my father was stubborn. "Someone has to stand up to them, though there are very few of us left." '

The MacKinnons made contact with three other families who had hidden when the brig was being loaded. They scoured the shore for timber for rafters, and cut new turf for the roof, having rebuilt the walls of their habitations.

'What was Major Finlayson's reaction, Mr MacKinnon?' a Commissioner asked, after the clerk had brought him more ink for his quill.

'His factor came to see us and told us that we must think we had been very clever, defying the laird, but he would show us. He told us that from that day our rent was doubled. But of course we weren't getting an extra inch of ground.'

But the MacKinnons were not to be defeated.

'We must have brought two hundred creels of seaweed on our backs up the steep brae to put on the ground so that we would get the maximum crops,' Uisdean recalled. 'Even my little brothers and sisters had small baskets on their backs, and my mother always maintained that was why Mary was never able to have children.'

Somehow they fed themselves from the poor soil, and coaxed from it surplus produce which they sold down in the town.

'So your family survived, Mr MacKinnon?'

'We did, and we began to hear news of those who had crossed the sea to a new life in Canada. We heard that twenty, including two babies, had died on the crossing in a boat that had twenty times as many rats as passengers, and that when our kinsfolk eventually reached Nova Scotia, the parcels of land they had been granted were not as generous as those forced on the emigrant brig

stories from an island   153

– I will not call them settlers, because that implies free will – had been led to believe, and that timber for making houses did not grow in the vicinity, but had to be hauled considerable distances. We also heard the land was poor, and that wheat did not have the yield that had been promised. There was also disease that took many lives, and I believe that broken hearts carried off many.'

But it wasn't much better on the island. The families who had refused to go on the emigrant brig had expanded, but the laird wouldn't grant them extra ground, and continued to push up the rents which they were unable to pay. In 1862 a poorhouse had been built to accommodate the destitute, and it was soon crowded.

In 1874 Ainsworthy the shipping magnate had bought the estate that included part of the town, and though Uisdean MacKinnon did not say so to the Commissioners, it seemed ironic that the money for this purchase should have come in part from shipping emigrants – most of them reluctant – from the Highlands and Islands to the new world. Enchanted with his Hebridean domain, Ainsworthy had reconstructed the original MacLean mansion house across the bay in elaborate Gothic style, as well as paying plant hunters to bring him back exotic specimens, particularly rhododendrons, from China and Tibet.

But the other half of the town where the MacKinnon croft was located was still owned by Major Finlayson, who had hired a noted Scottish Baronial architect to build him a new castle overlooking the open Atlantic five miles north from the town. His wife insisted that a former crofting township whose inhabitants her husband had forced on to the emigrant brig had to be demolished, since it interfered with the view from her boudoir. The Finlaysons' factor continued to harass the crofters, fining them for gathering firewood and increasing their rents.

'Major Finlayson will die a tyrant,' was Uisdean MacKinnon's last pronouncement before he bowed to the Commissioners, having taken nearly two hours to present his evidence.

A month later, he received notice from the factor to quit because of his 'hostile' evidence. However, he was determined to fight this injustice, and took his case to the courts in Edinburgh, where his impressive figure and clarity of presentation convinced the judge that he had been victimised, and the eviction order was quashed.

In 1892 Major Finlayson, aged ninety two, died of a seizure during a night of ferocious storm, when the ocean swamped the basement of his castle. His son, who had little interest in his island inheritance, put the estate on the market. Since he already had a fine residence surrounded by exotic plants, Ainsworthy only offered for the Finlayson land, ending up with over twenty thousand acres, which included the entire town and perhaps fifty crofts. Finlayson's castle, with its panoramic view of the Atlantic where his emigrant brig had sailed with its human cargo in the hold, was sold to a recently ennobled Englishman.

Uisdean's son, also Uisdean (the name to be perpetuated with pride in the family in honour of the patriarch), a volunteer in Princess Louise's Argyll and Sutherland Highlanders, was downed by a Boer bullet while trying to cross the Modder River in South Africa in 1900. However, Corporal Uisdean MacKinnon had married and left issue, an infant son, also Uisdean, as well as two daughters.

Uisdean MacKinnon the patriarch, eloquent champion of crofters' rights, died peacefully by his own fireside, in the company of his settled family in 1913, at the age of seventy seven, secure in the tenancy of the croft. In 1914 three of his grandsons sailed on the steamer to fight in the Great War. Andrew died at Festubert in 1915; shell-shocked on the Somme, Gilleasbuig was brought home on a stretcher and was to lie shaking day and night in his bed for the rest of his life.

Uisdean, son of the Boer War casualty, had lied about his age in his desire to enlist (he was only sixteen but looked like a man). He was promoted to Corporal like his father and received the Military Medal for 'conspicuous bravery' at Third Ypres, having run across open terrain to lob a grenade into a lethal machine gun nest.

Corporal Uisdean MacKinnon MM married a local girl, Raonaid (Rachel) and had five children. Uisdean kept two cows on the croft, to supply the household with milk, and to sell the surplus, in the form of cheese which Raonaid made, to the town. Uisdean supplemented this meagre income by working part-time as a stevedore down on the pier, unloading the cargo boats and steamers. In the winter this involved labouring in the darkness by the flickering light of lanterns, as sacks of flour and other provisions were swung ashore in a sling on the derrick.

This Uisdean was a gifted Gaelic singer who performed at ceilidhs in the hall that Colonel Ainsworthy had erected, and who also wrote Gaelic songs about the island, in particular the heartache of exiles. One song spoke of the anguish of an islander who had been shipped out to Nova Scotia on the emigrant brig, knowing that she would never see her beloved home again. The song was printed in Glasgow, together with the tune that Uisdean had composed, and became very popular at ceilidhs in that city.

Uisdean died of peritonitis in 1938, brought on, his family believed, by lifting too heavy sacks in the pier store. In 1940 his son Uisdean, aged twenty, was called up to serve in the navy. Like his father he had a talent for writing Gaelic songs, and tried to compose one about being on the deck of a destroyer accompanying a convoy through mountainous seas, but he couldn't find words to describe the breath of those watching out for U-boats turning into ice on their lips.

On the night that Uisdean's ship was torpedoed on a crossing to Halifax, Nova Scotia, his wife Beathag whom he had put in the family way when they were both aged eighteen, dreamed of him, but he was not foundering in the oil-sheened waves. Instead he was home on the family croft, his sleeves rolled up to his elbows on a golden afternoon as he scythed the fragrant hay with a blade that seemed to have been hammered out of the sun. For weeks after his loss his brothers took their boat round the coast of the island, in case his body had been washed into one of the innumerable inlets.

Uisdean's son, also Uisdean, was four years old when his father died. By the time he was eight he was milking the cows in the dawn and delivering the cheese after school. He also learned how to use a scythe, though his mother was always apprehensive that the blade would gash his legs. Uisdean wrote with his left hand, but this infuriated his teacher, who tied the boy's left arm up behind his back with a hay rope so that he would be forced to write with his free hand, or be belted on the same hand for refusing to use it. When he came home with the wrist of his right hand black and blue from the belt, his mother took him up to Dr Murdoch, who went round to the school and warned the teacher that he could be prosecuted for bodily injury.

Uisdean left school as soon as he could to help his mother Beathag on the croft. Since there wasn't enough income from the family croft he got a job in the local garage which was getting busier because of the increasing number of vehicles on the island. Uisdean trained as a mechanic, and had the uncanny knack of diagnosing an engine's fault simply by listening. At night, after he had shed his oil-stained boiler suit, he went out to work the croft.

Dressed in an old sweater and corduroys, Uisdean is standing, on any evening in the 1950s, in a corner of the field with the two cows, their brown and white dappled backs lit up by the sun that will shortly sink into the sea to the west of this blessed isle. It's hard to believe that on these peaceful acres, horsemen hired by the laird demolished the old house, its successor now used as a byre. It's as if the harrowing history of this little corner, with its reputed holy well from which the cattle drink, has been overwritten by peace.

Uisdean MacKinnon died on a September evening in 1964 when the jack slipped and the car came down on him. It's said that in times of crisis, people acquire superhuman strength, but not even the combined efforts of the other two mechanics, an apprentice, and two passers-by, could lift the vehicle (a Daimler belonging to the laird) from Uisdean's crushed chest. Dr Murdoch came down to pronounce him dead, then drove up the brae to break the news to Uisdean's wife Marion and his mother Beathag.

Uisdean's eldest son (what else but Uisdean?) was an assistant in Black's shop on Main Street when his father was killed. Though Uisdean gave his pay packet intact to his mother at the end of the week, Marion couldn't raise three children on her widow's pension and the paltry income from the family croft, where her mother-in-law Beathag was still living, so she took a job as a waitress in the Hebridean Hotel, but that entailed getting home late in the summer, when her children were already in bed.

Marion MacKinnon didn't have the money to renovate the old croft house, so she applied for and was allocated one of the new council houses that had been built at the top of the town, where the road turns south for the rest of the island. Beathag went with her, and what a blessing it was to have water from a tap and light from a switch, an electric cooker, a bath to relax in. Marion kept on the family croft, but sold the two cows, allowing a neighbour to keep his beasts on the ground for a nominal rent.

Marion's son Uisdean was a gentle person who kept a pencil behind his ear and who wore a brown overall. He was courteous with the customers, always enquiring about their families as he put the pound of nails or bottle of whisky in front of them.

One afternoon a girl from Glasgow who was staying for the summer with her aunt, came into Black's for a bottle of malt whisky which she wanted to send to her father for his birthday. Uisdean carefully wrapped the gift in corrugated paper, assuring her that it wouldn't break in the post.

The following week they were observed walking hand in hand across the golf course, and a few nights after that, Uisdean took her up to show her the family croft.

'It's such a beautiful spot, it's a pity you can't do up the house,'

Annabel remarked as they leaned over the fence.

'Even with grants going it's too expensive,' Uisdean told her. 'Besides, there's a problem. The laird wants it back.'

'What do you mean – wants it back?'

'His lawyers wrote to my mother, saying that since we're no longer occupying the house, he wants it and the land back. The letter said that the deeds his lawyers have in Edinburgh prove that we don't have a right to the ground under crofting law, so he's taking it back.'

'Surely you won't let him,' Annabel said, her father having marched in Glasgow with the great John McLean, the Communist agitator.

'We can't do very much about it,' Uisdean told her. 'We don't have the money to fight it in court.'

The following month one of the Ainsworthy estate workers cut the fence surrounding the croft and drove a mechanical shovel in, proceeding to demolish the house and the old byre, the habitation of the patriarch who had been so eloquent in front of the Napier Commission. The stones were loaded on to a lorry and taken across to Ainsworthy's mansion, where they were used as bottoming for the road to the jetty for his new motor yacht.

The first car ferry had already arrived on the island, ending the days of vehicles being swung one by one from the deck of the steamer by a derrick. The new ferry, whose bow opened up, was capable of carrying fifty vehicles, and by the end of that first summer the single-track roads were congested with cars and buses, the irate horns of the doctor and the postman demanding to get past. But the visitors refused to use the passing-places, and as a result, Dr Murdoch failed to reach Mrs Meg MacNicol on time to get her transferred to the mainland on the new ferry. Both she and her unborn baby died on the slow road down to the ferry terminal.

The summer after the MacKinnon croft had been cleared, the site was advertised in a glossy magazine which one of the maids in the Hebridean Hotel found in one of the bedrooms.

Annabel brought it down to read it out to Uisdean.

Highly desirable site for sale on a Hebridean island, with breathtaking views. The ground area will accommodate a substantial house, as well as an extensive garden. Water and electricity services will be provided by the vendors.

'Does it say the price?' Uisdean asked in dismay.

'No it doesn't. It says that prospective buyers are to contact a number in Edinburgh for a brochure,' Annabel told him. 'It's a bloody disgrace, taking the croft from you, then selling it.'

Uisdean decided not to show the magazine to his mother, because he knew it would upset her. He had other news for her: he and Annabel were getting engaged. They went to the mainland on the new car ferry to choose a ring with a single diamond within Uisdean's very limited budget.

On the day that he and Annabel were married in the parish church, with the reception in the Arms, followed by a dance in the hall, a couple drove their Jaguar off the car ferry and booked into the Hebridean Hotel. After afternoon tea in the conservatory they drove along the top of the town, past the parish church, outside of which the newly wedded couple were being bombarded with confetti, some of it clinging to the windscreen of the Jaguar as it continued up the hill to the MacKinnon croft. The man and woman opened the boot and changed into wellingtons before going to inspect the site.

'What a marvellous view!' the woman with the fancy English accent enthused, and her husband, equally fancy and wearing a deer-stalker, concurred. His green wellingtons paced out the site of a substantial house, while the woman laid out flower beds in her head. That evening before a seafood dinner they sent a telegram to the Edinburgh agents, making a bid for the croft site.

Next morning they went down to the bank, introducing themselves to Archie Maclean as Professor and Mrs Frogmore. He was about to retire from his Oxford chair and explained that they wanted a house in the Hebrides. However, they would retain their residence in Kent, which had a paddock and was listed as being of architectural merit.

'So you'll build here, if your offer is accepted,' the banker said cautiously.

'That's our plan,' Mrs Frogmore agreed.

'Have you taken into account that though this island is beautiful in this weather, in the winter it can be a depressing place buffeted by gales?' the banker enquired.

'It'll only be a place for the summer,' the Professor explained. 'We have an apartment in Malta where we'll go for the winter.'

'Have you considered the costs of building a house on an island such as this?' Archie Maclean persisted. 'All material has to be brought from the mainland.'

'We've been looking at brochures, so we'll probably buy a house in kit form that we can adapt, and get local tradesmen to erect it,' Mrs Frogmore explained.

The banker was in a bad mood over supper that evening.

'We have two more white settlers coming,' he announced to his family. 'An Oxford professor and his wife, neither of whom I took to. They're hoping to buy the MacKinnons' old croft and erect a holiday house on it. This is what comes of opening up the island with the car ferry.'

'But they'll probably transfer their account to your bank,' his wife pointed out.

'I'd rather they remained down south with their money. Gaelic's weak enough on this island, but it's going to die out within my time if many more non-speakers arrive. This place will become like a Sussex seaside town rather than a Hebridean community.'

Alice could have replied that it wouldn't matter very much if Gaelic died, but she didn't want to inflame the situation further, since she was essentially a peacemaker. It didn't matter to her if it were native islanders or incomers she met on Main Street with her basket and dog, so long as they acknowledged her.

The Frogmores were successful in their bid for the croft site, and the following Spring a kit house arrived on a low-loader off the ferry, causing a long tail-back of traffic as it negotiated the winding single-track road to the town. With the assistance of a local squad the house of plywood buttressed with breezeblock went up in a couple of days, and had water and electricity within the week. The following month the Frogmores arrived in a new Land Rover to measure for carpets and curtains, and to give instructions to a local man about the lay-out of the garden.

Uisdean's and Annabel's firstborn was called Uisdean. He made his way to and from school past the Frogmores' house on the former croft of his family, and often saw Mrs Frogmore kneeling by a flower-bed with a trowel, wearing a broad-brimmed hat. She had made a feature of the ancient well in the corner, putting bricks round it.

When Uisdean moved up to the secondary school Mr Thomson the history teacher, one of the last people in the place to work a croft, talked about the history of the town, explaining how much of the land at the top had been divided into crofts.

'Your family had one,' he informed Uisdean.

'Where was it?' the boy asked, intrigued.

'Where Professor and Mrs Frogmore's house is, near the cemetery.'

That afternoon on his way home Uisdean lingered, looking over the wall, trying to imagine the land without the Frogmores' conspicuous house. That evening he quizzed his parents about the croft.

'It was taken from us years ago by the laird,' his father explained.

'Surely he couldn't do that,' the boy said earnestly.

'How can we stand up against the likes of Colonel Ainsworthy, when he's got legal advisors?' his mother asked rhetorically.

'But crofting law's supposed to give crofters protection,' Uisdean persisted. 'We had lessons in history on it from Mr Thomson. He was talking about the Clearances, and how people could be evicted until the crofting laws were brought in and gave them security of tenure. He showed me a book, with evidence that Uisdean MacKinnon gave to the Napier Commission in 1883. Mr Thomson said he was related to us, and that he helped to get the crofting laws established.'

'Never mind the crofting laws. Go and get on with your homework if you're to make something of yourself,' his mother advised.

He was a bright boy at school, and his teachers predicted that he could go on to university. He loved animals and wanted to be a vet, but had been warned that there were many competitors for the number of places at the vet schools, and that he would have to achieve the highest grades in his certificates.

Uisdean was six months from his Higher examinations when his father was diagnosed with cancer. Uisdean senior had to go down to Glasgow to have surgery, but the X-rays showed that the cancer was extensive in both lungs, though he had never been a smoker.

Since Annabel had to look after the rest of the family, Uisdean junior stayed with an aunt and went to see his father every day in the Infirmary. He sat by his father's bed, reassuring him that he would soon be home, but saw the terror in his parent's face, and heard how difficult it now was for him to get breath. When his father was put into an oxygen tent Uisdean sat beside it until he died, and after that there was the sadness of having to accompany his father's remains home by train, sitting in the van with the coffin, and then helping to shoulder it aboard the car ferry.

Because of his father's illness and death Uisdean had lost a lot of time to study for his examinations. But he also knew that he couldn't go to university now, because there were still two siblings below him, and he would have to earn money to help his mother to bring them up, though she insisted that she would manage if he went to university.

The Frogmores' garden was now well established, with shrubberies and flower beds. They came up from the south from Easter until September, and during this time participated in local affairs. Professor Frogmore, who had been an archaeologist at Oxford, discovered human bones in a corner of his land. The sergeant was called, in case there had been a crime, but when the bones were sent to Edinburgh for analysis, it turned out that they belonged to a young girl who had died at least a hundred years before. The bones of Iseabail, sister of the patriarch Uisdean MacKinnon, were interred in an unmarked plot in the cemetery, across the road from the family croft.

Mrs Frogmore entered her plants for the annual show in the hall, and was consistently successful. She played the oboe, and, with other incomers, formed a quartet which performed in each others' houses. The Professor also tried to start a philatelic society, but there were very few enthusiasts on the island.

Uisdean MacKinnon, dux of the school, was working as a waiter in the Hebridean Hotel. The hours were long, but the tips from visiting yachtsmen were generous. What he didn't give to his mother he saved, because the hotel closed in the winter, and he would be out of work, unless he could find odd jobs.

In July one of three Italian waiters recruited by the hotel through a London agency had a tantrum, throwing a meat cleaver at one of the staff. He had to be repatriated, and a replacement found quickly. A waitress answered an advertisement in a Glasgow newspaper. Helen MacArthur was a shy, personable girl who found it difficult hoisting the plates above vulnerable heads as she steered between the tables in the Hebridean.

Many of the residents returned for the same fortnight in July, year in year out, and they expected preferential service. The result was that Helen became very nervous, and one evening an egg mornay ended up in the lap of the wife of a Chief Constable. The woman rounded on Helen, accusing her of clumsiness and warning her that she would be sent the account for cleaning the garment when the Chief Constable and his entourage went home.

Helen was crying in the staff hall when Uisdean MacKinnon came in, and in comforting her he put an arm round her shoulders. This was the start of a romance during which the young woman's confidence improved to the extent that she seemed to glide with the hot dishes among the tables.

At the end of September, when the hotel closed for the winter, Helen should have returned to Glasgow. But she had missed a period, and Dr Mary Fielding confirmed that she was pregnant. Instead she moved in with Uisdean's mother, and he supported her as well through a variety of jobs – serving petrol at the garage where his grandfather had been crushed under the laird's Daimler; helping in the public bar in the Arms at the weekend, when the fishermen came in to pour their catches down their throats.

The baby was born in April, in the week that the Hebridean Hotel opened for the season. He was christened Uisdean, and his proud father went about with a song in his heart in the re-painted dining-room of the hotel as he served the Easter visitors. In the evening as soon as the last person had left the dining-room – which could be very late, with people ordering yet another bottle of wine – he ran home to see his son, past the Frogmores' house, where the lights were on, because they had come up from the south for the Spring and summer.

On his day off Uisdean could be seen pushing his son's pram past the cemetery, with Helen walking beside him, her arm through his. As they went down the brae he explained that the Frogmores' house stood on a croft that had been in his family for generations.

It is not known why Uisdean's wife fell out with her mother-in-law. Perhaps it was because the baby cried during the night, and Helen had to get up to fix him a bottle. Perhaps it was the fact that there were four other persons in the house, and that Uisdean, his wife and baby were causing overcrowding. Whatever the reason, Uisdean decided to leave, and while he waited to get a house of his own he went into a caravan in Mrs Peggy MacQuade's garden at the top of the town.

Home to see her widowed mother and to hear her complaints about the weather, Marsaili Maclean met Uisdean on the brae and heard about his move, which she transmitted to her mother.

'I've heard about Peggy MacQuade's caravan in the hairdressers,' Alice told her daughter. 'It seems that it was one of the first made, and it arrived on this island on the old steamer. There's no water, no electricity, and there's a chemical toilet. If it was on the mainland it would be condemned, but here where the normal laws evidently don't apply, she can charge thirty pounds a week for a hovel on wheels.'

Marsaili knew that there wasn't any chance of Uisdean and his wife getting a council house, and there weren't any other houses for young married couples because as soon as a property came on the market, it was snapped up for a big price for a holiday home. She remembered her late father saying: 'When I think back to when we first came here, you could get a good cottage at the top of the town for a few thousand; now they're ten times that. The car ferry has been both a blessing and a curse, a blessing in that it has brought new business to this island, and a curse because it has brought the white settlers who've bought up all the houses. Then there are the settlers who have built houses by buying up croft land.'

'Which the locals sold to them,' Alice had pointed out to him.

'That's correct,' her husband agreed. 'I've seen many examples of greed in my time in the bank here. I've had old women in, with plenty in their account already, pleading with me to find a way to change their sister's will so that they can inherit her money too. But if people see so much money being spent on holiday homes, of course they'll want a share of it, which is why they get their ground decrofted, and then sell it, because of course they have a house already themselves.'

Marsaili felt sorry for Uisdean MacKinnon. He was a decent

person who could have gone on and qualified as a vet as she had done, but instead had stayed to support his mother when his father died, and was now supporting a wife and child. Marsaili knew that if she were in his position, she would feel very angry.

Uisdean certainly was angry, in the freezing caravan in the winter. The gas heater with the cylinder couldn't keep it warm because of the flimsy walls, and the outside tap from which he drew water was frozen, and even when he wrapped a newspaper round the tap and lit it, the water still wouldn't run. Besides, the baby was developing a chest complaint. His parents kept him between them in the bed to try to keep him warm, but his coughing kept them awake all night.

Uisdean was at the end of his tether, short with customers in the garage when he came out to serve them petrol, and also short with his wife when he trudged up the hill with the bag of shopping, past the Frogmores' house, now closed for the winter. He wrapped the baby in a blanket and carried him up to the doctor, who sounded the child's chest and said that it was a bad case of bronchitis.

But that night the baby's temperature began to rise, though Uisdean had shouldered a new gas cylinder up the icy brae for the heater. His wife was crying as he ran out of the door and up the hill, turning into the dark driveway leading to the doctor's house and hammering on the door. The locum doctor from the mainland came to the door in his slippers and told Uisdean to come back in the morning during surgery.

Uisdean gripped him by the lapels of his jacket.

'My son's sick. You're coming down with me.'

Frightened of Uisdean's anger, the doctor fetched his medical bag and got his car out of the garage, though the caravan was only minutes down the road.

'It's pneumonia,' he pronounced, after applying the stethoscope to the burning chest.

'But you said it was bronchitis!' Uisdean shouted.

'It's gone into pneumonia,' said the doctor.

'You'll need to give him something for it,' Helen pleaded.

'I'll give him an aspirin.'

'Aspirin?' Uisdean practically screamed. 'What fucking good is aspirin?'

'It should bring down the temperature,' the doctor told him.

He crushed the tablet with the back of a spoon and fed it to the baby in a little water.

'This place is too cold,' the doctor said.

'We've nowhere else to go,' Uisdean pointed out.

'What about your mother's?'

'She's got a full house.'

'The baby needs heat if he's going to have a chance.'

'Why do you mean – have a chance?' Helen asked fearfully.

'He's very ill. If it had been daylight I would have sent him to hospital on the mainland, but a helicopter can't land here in the darkness. I'll order one first thing in the morning.'

'What if I asked one of the fishermen to take him to the mainland in his boat?' Uisdean suggested desperately.

'It would be too cold for him. He needs to stay in the warmth. I would take him up to my house, but it's too risky, even for the short journey. Can't you get another heater?'

'This caravan doesn't have electricity,' Uisdean informed him.

'Will the owner have a heater?'

'Mrs MacQuade is too mean. I'll go and see if anyone can lend me one.'

'Call me if there is any change,' the doctor said. 'Put this on him,' he added, taking off his coat.

Uisdean went round half a dozen doors that night, but either the people were in bed and wouldn't answer, or they didn't have a gas heater, since by this time most of the houses in the town were centrally heated. He was so distraught that he ran up the brae, shouting curses on the town and its people, asking why he and his family had arrived in such a situation.

Helen was desperately trying to keep the baby warm with her

body heat in the freezing caravan, but she noticed towards dawn that he had become cold. The father was frantically massaging the feet, but the heart had stopped.

In a town such as this, stories passing into folklore become distorted, sometimes out of all proportion. This is partly the fault of the remnants of the Gaelic oral tradition, where every person who relays a story feels that he or she has to embellish it to make it more interesting. The trouble with this is that in such reworking of tales, the innocent become the guilty and vice versa.

When the child's coffin came off the car ferry, Uisdean insisted on carrying the small white box up to the cemetery himself, instead of having it conveyed by the local hearse. The grave overlooked the old MacKinnon croft on which the Frogmores' holiday house now stood, and as the Minister intoned 'dust to dust, ashes to ashes,' sprinkling the frost-hardened soil on the white box below, Uisdean was standing, holding Helen's hand as if the force of their grief was about to precipitate them into the grave with their son. There had not been such a harrowing funeral in living recollection.

That evening the phone rang in the house of Angus Livingstone, the volunteer firemaster on the island, informing him that flames had been seen coming from the Frogmores' house. By the time the eight volunteers had pulled on their uniforms and opened the doors of the fire station, the house was well alight.

They lifted the cover on the road below the cemetery, but the fire hydrant had frozen, and by the time they had a supply rigged up through the window of a nearby house, the Frogmores' roof had collapsed. Despite the force of the hose the property was gutted within the hour.

Next morning the sergeant went into the smouldering ruins with the firemaster in an attempt to find out what had caused the blaze. The heat was coming up through their soles as they examined the blackened tangle of wires for an electrical fault. Certainly the electricity had been left on, because the Frogmores kept minimum heat in their property throughout the winter to stop dampness.

The following day an insurance assessor drove off the car ferry and spent the rest of the day in the ruins, before putting something into the boot of his vehicle (the inquisitive Mrs Annie Robertson couldn't see what it was from her window) and driving up to the police station.

Uisdean knew the sergeant would come and was waiting for him with a full confession. Next morning, he was taken away handcuffed on the car ferry. The case was too serious to be tried locally, so it went to Glasgow. Marsaili took time off from her busy practice to go and listen to the evidence, but really to give Uisdean support. The Frogmores were there, out for revenge, though their property had been well insured. Uisdean conducted his own defence, and spoke as eloquently and passionately as his ancestor, also Uisdean MacKinnon, had done before the Napier Commission over a century before.

'The laird claimed the croft that we had worked for as long as anyone could remember, and sold it to white settlers to build a fancy house on. My wife, my baby and myself had to live in a caravan because we had nowhere else to go. Then my son died of pneumonia because of the cold. Yes, I burned down the Frogmores' house, not only for revenge, but because I wanted to make a statement about the number of houses on the island that have become holiday homes, depriving young people of the chance to settle down and raise families.'

Marsaili could see from the expressions of both the jury and the judge that they were moved by his plight. She expected that he would get a lenient sentence, but the prosecutor rose to ask the accused a final question.

'Does this mean that you would set fire to other holiday houses?'

'Yes it does,' said Uisdean. 'I would like to burn out the white settlers as my people were burned out in the Clearances.'

Uisdean MacKinnon was found guilty and given five years. He

was in Barlinnie Prison in Glasgow, and when she had free time, Marsaili used to visit him. She told him that with good behaviour he would earn remission, and that he should think about making a new life for himself in Glasgow.

'Perhaps you could train as a veterinary assistant. I can certainly give you work,' she promised him.

Helen moved to Glasgow, to be near her husband. But it was a long wait, and she met someone else in a café on Byres Road. After his release it is thought that Uisdean emigrated, possibly to Canada.

15
The Cradle of Life

When Marsaili Maclean was in school in the town there was no Gaelic in the primary classes, but now a Gaelic medium school had been established, and when she was up on holiday and was out for an early walk she would meet a child going up the brae with his mother, and the boy would call '*madainn mhath!*' to her, which Marsaili thought was charming.

This was Diarmid MacMillan, the son of Murchadh, which was how he rendered his name Murdo, after being one of only two persons of his generation from the town to study Gaelic at university, having been awarded first class honours in Celtic at Aberdeen University.

Being a learner, Murchadh was dedicated to the language. It is said that when Murchadh went to a dance in the hall and took a fancy to one of the girls, his first question wasn't 'Would you like to dance?' but '*A bheil Gàidhlig agad?*' which made most of the girls giggle and avoid this earnest linguist, who apparently had only one topic of conversation.

Marsaili didn't like meeting Murchadh because she felt that their conversation became a test of her competency in Gaelic, and she began to lose confidence in her grasp of the grammar of the language which she had learned with the assistance of her father, and of old people in the town who couldn't read or write Gaelic, but whose conversations were very evocative, full of colloquialisms, however quaint the grammar.

When Robertson retired Murchadh became the Gaelic teacher in the secondary school. He insisted on using only Gaelic with his pupils, when they had covered very little vocabulary. Also, he gave them more homework than any other teacher, insisting on two ink exercises per week. He was a hard marker, especially when accents were missing.

A young woman called Catherine Sinclair came to teach English in the school, and on her first day when Murchadh met the attractive incomer in the corridor he welcomed her to the island in Gaelic and was surprised to receive an acknowledgement in the same language. She explained that her parents came from the island of Barra and had spoken Gaelic to her as a child.

'But I can't read or write it,' she confessed.

'I'll teach you,' he offered, and even before lessons got underway he had proposed.

Within a year of their marriage they had a son, and even before the midwife had cut the cord the father was speaking to him in Gaelic. When he informed Catherine that they would speak only Gaelic with their son for the first few years, she protested.

'But my Gaelic's not good enough. It's only conversational.'

'I can help you to improve it,' her husband offered.

'I'm not sure that I want to improve it.'

Murchadh was horrified by this admission, because he had already written out a lesson plan to teach her to read and write the language he held so dear.

'But we'll be depriving the boy of his heritage.'

'His heritage has already disappeared in this town,' Catherine reminded him. 'I can go for days without hearing a word of Gaelic on Main Street. If Diarmid's going to get on he's going to have to speak English.'

'What do you mean – get on?' her husband asked truculently.

'I mean, get on in the world. Everyone uses English, wherever you go – even abroad. You're a Gaelic romantic, Murchadh.'

After further heated discussion they agreed a compromise: Catherine would speak Gaelic with the boy, if Murchadh spoke with their son for part of the time in English. Murchadh had to agree, though he was angry, and when he was left alone with the boy he only spoke to him in Gaelic.

One afternoon he came in from school in a state of excitement.

'They're going to set up a Gaelic medium unit.'

'What does that mean?' she asked suspiciously.

'It means that Diarmid's going to be taught through Gaelic in the primary school,' he told her triumphantly.

'No English?' his wife said, alarmed.

'What's the point in that if he's learning Gaelic? It will only confuse him.'

By the time the 1990s ended the number of native speakers in the town could be counted on the fingers of both hands, and only two of them were under fifty. These figures saddened Marsaili, considering her late father's commitment to Gaelic, but then, for a variety of reasons, the language had been in decline on the island since the 1930s. Teachers with no knowledge of, or tolerance for Gaelic had come from the mainland. But that wasn't the full story. Some of those who had taken in the language with their mothers' milk wouldn't speak it, because they worked in shops and hotels, and the visitors wouldn't understand them, or perhaps feel insulted. Then again, if staff in a big house were caught speaking Gaelic, it was assumed that they were criticising their English employers, and it was said (though never confirmed, like so many stories on the island) that a maid at a shooting lodge in the south of the island had actually been dismissed for asking another servant for a cigarette in Gaelic.

Even when Marsaili was a girl learning Gaelic, very few of her own generation spoke the language. She was fortunate because she could have natural conversations in the language with her father, but others of her peer group who might be anxious to improve their spoken Gaelic would have had to go up and sit with old people. The generation gap was too big and besides, the Sea Breezes Café had a jukebox. Who wanted to listen to Neil Maclean singing 'The Dark Stream' when for a shilling you could hear Elvis serenading his blue suede shoes?

Then the Gaelic medium unit was started, and old women stopped Diarmid on the street and gave him fifty pence for speaking Gaelic with them because by the time he was five he was fluent. Marsaili herself had conversations with him when she met the boy and his father on the brae, and felt that Diarmid's Gaelic was probably better than her own.

The exact date of the arrival of the first jukebox on the island can easily be pinpointed, because a photograph exists of the box, shrouded in sacking, being swung off the cargo boat from Glasgow on to a lorry for conveyance to the Sea Breezes Café, where an electric plug had already been installed for it.

Computers soon became as common as cats in the town and even children had them in their bedrooms in converted lofts. But not Diarmid MacMillan. His father, whose skills in do-it-yourself equalled his skills in Gaelic, had fitted out the loft for his son. There was a Velux rooflight which, Murchadh insisted, was to be left open at night so that his boy could grow big and strong on the breezes from the bay, like his Celtic antecedents. Some nights, when a stiff westerly was blowing, Catherine had to leave her bed and come up the narrow staircase to shut the rooflight above her shivering son.

Murchadh had made a shelf beside the boy's bed so that his

Gaelic books were within easy reach, with a little lamp beside. However, there was no small television set, as there were in the bedrooms of so many children throughout the town, because it was a way of keeping them quiet, out of sight, allowing their parents below to follow Brookside undisturbed.

When Gaelic children's programmes came on, Diarmid was expected to join his father at the television set downstairs, and afterwards he was tested on what he had learned from the programme. If he got all the answers right he was given a bar of honey and crushed peanuts, because that was good for his health. For Christmas, when his friends were receiving the latest computer games they had ordered from Santa, using their parents' credit cards, Diarmid found a Gaelic video on top of his small pile of presents on Christmas morning, while Gaelic carols played on a tape below.

Many people in the town wondered how on earth someone like Bobby Dobson had managed to get into the Gaelic medium unit. His father Andy had come to the island from Glasgow twelve years before to work. Having practically drunk dry the well-stocked gantry of the Arms, Andy had put one of the local girls in the family way. Three further children soon filled the council house at the top of the town. The springs of the sofa were exposed, the kids ran around half-naked, but the television set was never off. Even during the night when Andy was turning in drunken sleep, wondering if he should augment his family, the eerie blue beam of the set lit up the deserted room downstairs.

Bobby the firstborn was his father's favourite. Andy liked to finish an evening in the Arms by joining in the Gaelic singing at his habitual stance at the end of the counter, within convenient distance of the urinal, essential after ten pints.

This might have been what decided Andy to send Bobby to the Gaelic medium unit. If so, was it not a disastrous educational decision? His mother's family hadn't spoken Gaelic for two generations and even his father's English was unintelligible at times.

Bobby prospered in the Gaelic medium unit, perhaps not surprising, considering that he was exposed to the language from nine a.m. till three p.m. except for breaks in the playground, where the Gaelic scholars could join their English speaking peers in the other part of the school.

Diarmid became an admirer, then a friend of Bobby's. They sat across from each other in the classroom, vying as to who would get his hand up first to answer the question. They were also neck-and-neck in the points the teacher allocated for their written work. They walked home together – at least as far as the bridge, where Bobby turned left for the council houses and Diarmid proceeded to his terraced home in one of the streets laid out above the harbour in Victorian times.

'Do you like Gaelic?' Diarmid asked his friend in Gaelic one afternoon as they idled on the bridge, throwing stones into the sluggish water.

'Ask me in English,' Bobby prompted.

'Well – do you?'

'I fucking hate it.'

Diarmid was so appalled by the betrayal, he couldn't cast the next stone.

'Then why do you take it?'

'My Da wanted me to take it, so I said to him, "what's in it for me?" He offered me two pounds a week but I said that wasn't enough, so we settled for three.'

'You get paid to go to the Gaelic unit?' Diarmid asked in bewilderment.

'Why do you go?'

'Dad wants me to be a Gaelic speaker.'

'Not a good enough reason,' Bobby concluded, shaking his head because he was old for his years. 'What do you get out of it?'

'Nothing,' his friend admitted. He found himself unable to use the word satisfaction, because it wasn't true and he was being brought up to be truthful.

'I fucking hate Gaelic too.'

As soon as he said this Diarmid expected heaven to fall on his head but nothing happened. So this time he shouted it out.

Bobby was grinning.

'You see, you're learning. Make it difficult for him.'

'Make what difficult for who?'

'For your old man. Tell him that if you're going to go on with this Gaelic crap, you've got to get something out of it. He'll see sense. I'm thinking myself of asking my Da for more money – maybe up to four quid. Disks are expensive.'

'What's that?'

'You don't know what a disk is?' Bobby said incredulously. 'Do you not have a computer at home?'

Diarmid shook his head.

'What kind of parents have you got? Tomorrow afternoon we'll go up to my house and I'll show you what a disk is.'

Bobby also lives in the loft of his house, but it isn't such a stylish conversion as Diarmid's and there isn't a shelf for Gaelic books. Instead of fixed stairs, Bobby has to pull down an aluminium ladder and once he and Diarmid are in the loft he pulls up the ladder and shuts the hatch.

The computer was being thrown out by a wealthy incomer who had decided to upgrade, when Andy stopped him carrying it (plus the printer) out to the bin. All that had to be bought was the joystick. As for the table the computer is resting on, Andy rescued it from a skip and repaired the leg.

The electricity supply is a lethal cable brought up through a crude hole in the ceiling from an overloaded socket below. The screen is illuminated, and Bobby, having shown his friend what a disk is, inserts it in the slot. This is the latest game that arrived this morning (£18 – six weeks of bribery money from the Gaelic medium unit).

The plot is simple. A half-naked girl is lost in a maze and a grotesque villain with designs on her has entered the maze. He will have to be taken out before he violates her. This is why the loft is full of bursts of light and sound as Bobby manipulates the joystick, firing off round after round, only to find that the villain has dodged down another path of the maze.

'Missed the bastard again!' Bobby yells. 'Do you want a shot?'

Diarmid's eyes are wide and shining in the illumination of the screen as he grasps the joystick, the bullets flashing like tracer. The villain is racing down another path, but this time it's a dead end and he writhes against the shrubbery in a hail of bullets, most realistic blood dripping from his wounds.

'Got the bastard!' the two boys sing together.

The villain is resurrected, to begin again his designs on the terrified virgin lost in the maze. The loft is full of blue light and blue language, not one word of it Gaelic.

'Bobby Dobson has asked me to his house next Friday night,' Diarmid announces to his parents.

'The Dobsons?' Catherine says, horrified. 'You can't go there. They say they live worse than the tinkers.'

'Don't miscall the tinkers,' her husband cautions her. 'They've made a big contribution to Gaelic culture.'

'Why do you turn everything into a lecture on Gaelic?' his wife rounds on him. 'I don't want Diarmid going to the Dobsons' house. The language of their kids is appalling. I heard them the other day with their mother in the Co-op.'

'I want to go to Bobby's because of Gaelic,' their son explains. 'We're top of the class together, and we can help each other.'

'Then you're going,' his father said decisively. 'Anything that improves your Gaelic is welcome.'

At this point Catherine went out, slamming the door.

stories from an island   179

There isn't a Gaelic book in sight in the Dobsons' loft, but there's a new disk that arrived in the morning post. Bobby got a DVD player for Christmas and has re-negotiated the levy from his father for attending the Gaelic medium unit. It's now up to five pounds a week to pay for DVD disks. ('You may as well give the money to the wee bugger,' Andy's wife said philosophically. 'You'll only piss it against a wall.')

Bobby slots in the DVD disk of *The Cradle of Life*, the first Lara Croft classic. Following an earthquake that exposes the lost site of the Lunar Temple of Alexander the Great, Lara arrives to find a glowing orb, but the temple is raided by Shai Ling bandits who seize the orb, leaving her to die. However, she escapes, to a great cheer from Bobby and Diarmid, who are wearing baseball caps and eating Mars Bars, though Diarmid's mother prohibits them because they are so bad for the teeth.

Back in England Lara is approached by MI6, who want her to stop international bio-weapons designer Jonathan Reiss, who is conducting an international auction of a deadly new virus.

'Reiss looks like that bastard Wilkinson, who teaches chemistry up in the big school!' Bobby yells.

Lara realises that the orb is a map that leads to Pandora's Box, the legendary Cradle of Life, from which human life originated but which also contains the potential to eliminate all life. She requests the freedom of her former lover, Scottish mercenary Terry Sheridan, from a Kazakhstan prison so that he can lead her to the Shai Ling base. Heading from China to Hong Kong to Africa, the two race to get to the Cradle and stop Reiss obtaining the virus.

The gorgeous Lara in her tight-fitting costume and funky belt is flying through the air to save the world. There are passionate kisses and a couple of bad words in the film, but Diarmid is enthralled and joins Bobby in yelling: 'Come on, Lara, kill that fucking wicked scientist!'

At nine thirty, when Diarmid is collected in the car by his father, the rooflight in Bobby's house is dark, the world saved, the delectable Lara abed.

'Well, how did your Gaelic session go?' Murchadh asks his son.

'Bobby knows more vocabulary than I do, Dad. We're going to meet again next Friday.'

'*Tha sin glè mhath gu dearbh*' (That's very good indeed), Murchadh says, starting the engine.

16
The Sunlit Eye

The field glasses that his father had picked up in the quagmire of Flanders were always on the window sill, so that if Hector saw a strange bird, he would reach for them. Beside the glasses was the bird identification book, its pages curled, some of them stained because he had hurried across from cooking at the stove on hearing a strange cry out at sea. Though his house on the headland wasn't sheltered, he loved storms, lying in the box-bed by the stove, listening to the wind rising, the spray hissing over his corrugated roof. One morning he had wakened to find seaweed draped round the door handle, like some strange ritual. He knew from Gaelic folklore that the sea has its gods, just like the land, and that they sometimes require offerings.

He would be up at first light after the gale, taking the field glasses outside and searching the sea for new arrivals. One dawn he had seen a raft of sooty shearwaters riding two hundred yards offshore. How had they managed to stay together throughout the storm, when there was the body of a guillemot at his boots, lifted from the trough of the waves and thrown ashore, its neck broken?

In the winter months he sat by the paraffin lamp, thumbing through Dwelly's dictionary, searching for the birds he had identified in order to discover their Gaelic names. Sometimes he found mistakes in the dictionary and noted them in the margin, beside the little drawing of the bird in question.

One morning he found a sandpiper on the shore, the ring-pull from a can round its bill. He took the whitened skeleton home and set it on the mantelpiece above the stove, touching it every time he passed it as if the slim bones would take flight again. Man killed more creatures than the worst weather.

He didn't need to listen to the radio or buy a newspaper to know about global warming. The west coast of the island was getting wetter and wetter, the ground waterlogged for weeks so that he couldn't plant his potatoes. One summer afternoon, scything the hay, he had seen a strange butterfly, and gone indoors to consult one of his books. It should have been confined to the south, but had migrated north as the climate changed. It was still there when he came out and it perched on the back of his hand, fanning its gorgeous yellow wings as if trying to cool down the doomed world.

Once a month he filled half a dozen buckets from the detritus he gathered on the shore. Why did water now need to come in plastic bottles? Condoms floated like a new species of jellyfish. He also collected pieces of timber seasoned in the ocean because he was a woodcarver. The birds he had carved were arranged on a shelf round the room. He had spent a winter shaping a curlew from a block of African mahogany, filing away at the long slender bill, suspending his breath in case it snapped. He had taken one of his works of art, a dunlin, to the English woman in the village who ran the bird club and needed items for a raffle.

'You could make a lot of money selling your carvings to tourists,' she advised him. 'I do very well myself, out of my macramé.'

He was a polite man and didn't say anything, though he knew

that there were far more incomers than natives on the island now. His parents had named the world around him in Gaelic, never using an English word when there was one available in their native tongue. But Gaelic was dying. Who now knew the various expressions for the various states of the sea? *An lear an saìmh shuain*, the sea in profound repose; *cuan salach nan garbh-thonn*, the troubled billowy sea; expressions that his father, a fisherman-crofter like himself, had used. Who now knew that the bog myrtle was called *eagach*, and that an infusion of its leafy tops used to be given to children as a remedy for worms? You got far worse than worms from hamburgers.

At the same time as plants and animals with Gaelic names were threatened through global warming, the Gaelic language was also in danger of extinction. Not that he had anybody to speak Gaelic with, both his parents now gone. A few years before he had gone on the ferry to the mainland for a medical examination and on the return journey had met an islander who had done well for himself. '*Ciamar a tha thu?*' Hector had greeted the man's teenage children and was appalled when they stared uncomprehendingly at him. Yet this man, who hadn't passed on his native language to his own children, was the son of literate native Gaelic speakers, his father a tradition-bearer.

Gaelic had been passed down through oral tradition. Like most of the older generation on the island Hector's parents had not been able to read and write Gaelic and he had had to teach himself by reading the Bible aloud, a dictionary by his other hand. But the oral transmission had now been broken. If Gaelic managed to survive in some form, it would be a different language, grammatically perfect perhaps, learnt through tapes and books and lacking the rich stories and allusions of the oral inheritance.

The Gaels blamed the education system and incomers for the decline of their language, but many of them were to blame themselves. Hector had met people who had denied knowing the language, yet he knew they were native speakers. They considered

Gaelic to be a backward language and didn't want to be heard speaking it. One woman had told him that she had felt 'illiterate' because she could only speak Gaelic, so she abandoned it, turning a blank face to a greeting in Gaelic, like the islander's children on the ferry.

One evening on his walk he saw a strange bird. It had alighted on a hillock, and he stood still, lifting his field glasses slowly, so as not to alert the creature. He had studied a picture of this bird many times in one of his books, but had never seen one before. He recognised the brown upper parts and chocolate-brown under-parts, the distinctive white tail of a sea eagle. His grandfather had taken him on his knee and told the boy in his expressive Gaelic about seeing the last pair of *iolair suìl na gréine* (the eagle with the sunlit eye) a year before the laird's brother had robbed the nest and shot both parents, sending them south to be stuffed.

Hector had heard on the radio that the bird had been re-introduced to the Hebrides from Scandinavia and that it was flourishing. He stood watching it feeding through his field glasses. He knew that it was a female because the book showed the female as being larger, the head darker than the male's. It was tearing its prey in its black claws before it rose on massive lethargic wings, wheeling towards the cliff where, his grandfather had informed him, the sea eagles had nested in the past before the laird's brother had blasted the majestic bird from the island.

Hector was back the next evening and this time he took a step closer to the feeding bird. It turned its head, the fierce eye watching him, but somehow it knew that he meant it no harm. He came out every evening in the fine weather for a month, latterly bringing a sketch pad with him as the eagle feasted on the hillock. Some nights its supper was a fish, other nights a hare or grouse.

Hector had been gifted in art at school, though there hadn't been any money for him to go on to college. He had pencils in the top pocket of his jacket and he pulled them out one by one as he coloured in the plumage, a yellow one for the bill. It was as if the female knew it was sitting for its portrait and it remained on the knoll, preening itself in its beauty and power, its wings spread like a cloak, a Renaissance princess.

On the last night he sketched it, Hector brought it a dead rabbit, because he had read in his book that sea eagles would eat carcasses. He threw the rabbit towards it, then retreated, watching the bird rising with the gift in its claws. He made a frame out of driftwood for his sketch, hanging it above the stove and would use it in winter to carve a likeness of the bird, as soon as the sea delivered a large enough block of wood.

He heard the male before he saw it, yelping above his head, so close to the sun, its white tail like a torch. Some nights the male came to fish in front of the house, as if putting on a demonstration for the diminutive figure with the field glasses among the lethal detritus on the shore. Hector watched it flying in, its yellowish white feet extended, its claws striking in an explosion of spray, the wriggling fish hoisted away.

Once a week Hector walked a mile to the van that stopped at the road end, where he bought items like sugar which he couldn't harvest himself from the land and sea.

'The sergeant was telling me that there's an egg thief on the island,' Alasdair the driver said.

Hector picked up his purchases and put them into the bag without comment.

'Evidently he's after the eggs of the sea eagle. Did you know there's a pair nesting in these parts?'

Hector shook his head.

What is this man interested in? the driver asked himself. *Just look at the state of his clothes. I've seen tinkers better dressed. He must have a lot of money hoarded in that house of his.*

He was cutting peats at the bank near his house one evening when he saw a figure in the distance. It was a man, with binoculars with which he was scanning the landscape. He was too close to the knoll where the sea eagles came to feed, so Hector knew that he had to do something about it. He thrust his spade into the glistening black bank of peat and crossed the moor to the stranger.

'Are you lost?' Hector enquired.

'I don't think so,' the man said in an English voice, taking an Ordnance Survey map from the pocket of his waxed jacket. 'I'm here, amn't I?' he said, stabbing a finger.

'Yes you are,' Hector said cautiously.

'I'm a bird watcher,' the stranger said. 'I'm particularly interested in seeing a sea eagle. Have you seen the pair that's about in these parts?'

'I wouldn't know what a sea eagle looked like,' Hector told him.

The man was surveying Hector, from his cap to his wellingtons, coming to the conclusion that here was a simpleton.

'It's a big bird, with a wing-span like this,' the stranger persisted, opening his arms to their full extent.

Hector pushed back his cap and scratched his forehead.

'I've never seen a bird that size before,' he said, in a tone which suggested he didn't believe it were possible.

Hector stood for a long time watching until the stranger was out of sight. Even from a distance he had seen by the way the man held his binoculars, with his elbows sticking out, that he wasn't a bird watcher.

Every night Hector was out with his field glasses, but he wasn't looking for the eagles with the sunlit eye. He was looking for the stranger. A week later he had him in focus, descending the cliff where the sea eagles had nested in the past. He crossed the moor and stood at the bottom of the cliff, and when the climber was on the ground again he pointed his shotgun at the man.

'Empty your pockets,' he ordered.

The man reached into his inside pocket and produced a wad of notes, peeling off fifty pounds and handing them to Hector.

'This is for not saying anything.'

The notes dropped at Hector's boots and fluttered away on the breeze.

'Empty your pockets,' Hector repeated.

The thief laid the two rough white eggs, without gloss, on the heather. Hector took them and put them inside his shirt, close to his heart.

'Take off your jacket – and your shirt.'

The stranger looked at the gun, then began to undress.

'Tear that up into strips,' Hector ordered, pointing the barrels at the shirt.

The man ripped it apart.

'Now wrap these carefully in it,' Hector instructed, handing him the eggs one by one. 'They're still warm and you're going to put them back.'

'I'm not going back up there,' the egg thief protested. 'It's too bloody dangerous.'

'Then I'll shoot you,' Hector told him factually, in his soft voice.

The thief started climbing, bare-chested in the chilly evening. He kept looking down, but the man had the barrels pointing up. Then Hector lifted the field glasses from the carnage of Flanders round his neck and watched the climber approaching the nest on the ledge. He reached up and put the eggs in, one by one.

The egg thief was on his way back down when the female arrived and began to beat his head with its massive wings as it yelped like a wounded dog. Through the field glasses Hector watched the thief falling, the body thudding into the heather, the skull splitting open against a rock. He could have gone home for a spade, but decided to leave the corpse there.

The ravens would take the predatory eyes, and when the remains started rotting the offspring of the eagles with the sunlit eyes might be tempted. One thing was certain: no one would come looking for the stranger in this remote spot.

That winter a massive tree trunk came ashore, and Hector knew he had the wood for the carving of the sea eagle, which would take him a year. By the time he had finished the beak the two eagle chicks were fishing offshore.

17
Lofty Ambitions

Dr Murdoch was tired. He had been down the island that stormy day, attending a dying patient and was delayed on his way back by a tree across the road which had to be hauled clear by two plough horses in chains. It meant that he was late for evening surgery. He was just sitting down to his late supper when a phone call from a box in the town asked him to come quickly because Meg Mac-Dougall's baby was on its way. When the doctor came down he saw that it was a breech birth and in trying to bring the reluctant head out into the light of the world he damaged the skull with forceps, so that an old woman in the town, seeing the two score marks, would say that it was the devil's hoof mark.

Lachlan was a very docile baby who gave his mother no trouble. But it was obvious that he was retarded, either because of the clumsy forceps or because there had been 'oddities' (Gille Ruadh's word) in the families before, and in particular an uncle, who believed that he was Field Marshal Haig and who ended his days in an asylum on the mainland.

Lachlan's father was a skilled carpenter who was carried home one day when the boy was six. He had fallen from the roof of the Free Church manse and was in too much pain from his fractured spine to be sent to the mainland. He slept away on the massive amounts of morphine that Dr Murdoch gave him.

Lachlan didn't speak till he was six and by the time he left primary school he still couldn't read. Dr Murdoch suggested sending him to a special school on the mainland, but his mother wouldn't hear of it. She was determined to keep him at home, to give him the best chance. After the age of twelve he didn't return to school, but the whipper-in, who pursued other truants on his bicycle, left Lachlan alone, probably because he realised that there was no benefit to be had in the simple boy going to school.

However, he was good with his hands and his mother tacked his drawings up on the kitchen wall. She had bought him a little carpentry set for his Christmas and though the saw wasn't sharp, and the hammer was light, he had made a little plywood box for her. She didn't know what he expected her to keep in it, since she had no jewellery or other adornments. She kept it beside her bed, and every night, when she said her prayers, this devout mother had the box in her hands. After all, Jesus had been a carpenter and he must have looked after his apprentices.

She spoke to MacDiarmid the boatbuilder, the last on the island, and he took Lachlan on, giving him ten shillings a week for holding the lengths of wood to be steamed into the ribs of the boat he was building for Colonel Ainsworthy as a tender for his yacht. MacDiarmid was a decent man, but didn't feel able to give Lachlan more responsibility, because wood was expensive and it was difficult to undo a mistake in a boat, especially when the client was the local laird. After a year Lachlan, who had had limited attention-span in school, seemed to lose interest in learning the craft of boat building and didn't turn up one Monday morning.

He remained at home with his mother, who got a small allowance for him, because he was classified as disabled. They had no rent to pay because the house had been built by Lachlan's grandfather, a master carpenter who had made the grand staircase for the Victorian castle in the far north of the island and who had taken the same care with the woodwork of his own modest abode. Lachlan grew vegetables in their garden and was given odd jobs about the town by people who felt sorry for him, including the bank manager, who asked him to cut the small hedge in front of the property and who came out to converse with him in Gaelic. Lachlan was a very shy person and while he was talking to you he would look away, as if he felt he looked peculiar.

'It's a great shame about him because he's got such good Gaelic,' Archie Maclean told his wife. 'I must try to find him odd jobs.'

'Please don't ask him to do anything in this house,' Alice pleaded.

'Why not?'

'Because he looks so clumsy, the way he walks along the street, as if he's going to bump into everybody. There's something wrong with his co-ordination.'

'That's because he was delivered by Dr Murdoch.'

One afternoon Mrs MacDougall heard hammering at the back of the house and went out to investigate.

'What's that you're making?' she asked Lachlan.

'A ladder.'

'Surely you're not going to go up on the roof,' she said in terror, after what had happened to his father.

'I'm going up into the loft.'

'What for? There's nothing in it, as far as I know.'

But he continued to hammer slats of wood into a ladder. She let him bring it into the house, up his grandfather's beautifully finished staircase and on to the landing. He took a torch with him before he ascended, lifting aside the perfectly fitted hatch.

'What can you see?' his mother called anxiously from the bottom of the ladder.

'Nothing but cobwebs. And bats,' he called back in Gaelic.

'Bats?' she said apprehensively. 'How are they getting in?'

'I can see light coming through the gable,' he reported back. 'I'll nail a board to keep them out.'

'Don't shut them in, whatever you do.'

He seemed to be spending every day up in the loft, carrying boards up on his shoulder, as if he were replacing the entire roof. But she left him to it, because the ladder he had built seemed sturdy and because it was keeping him occupied and giving him the satisfaction of doing something useful. But when she saw him carrying a paraffin lamp up his ladder, she stopped him.

'You can't take that up there,' she said, horrified. 'You'll set fire to the place.'

He descended and set the lamp back on the table, but two days later, asked her for money to buy new batteries for the torch.

'Are you not finished up there?' she asked him one morning, because his hammering into the small hours was keeping her awake.

'It's a bigger job than I thought.'

Then she heard him going out the door at night. She lay awake for hours, until she heard him coming in before dawn.

'Where have you been?' she challenged him.

'I went for a walk.'

'At *this* hour?'

He produced the torch from his pocket. She was worried that he was doing something out there in the darkness that would get him into trouble with the law and have him taken away from her, to an institution on the mainland, like his uncle.

'I don't want you going out at night,' she told him.

'I'm not doing any harm,' he protested.

The next night she lay listening, but the stairs had been so well made that she didn't hear him going down and out of the front door, carrying his boots until he was clear of the house, then descending the brae. That was when the banker and Gille Ruadh met him, on their way up the brae after the telephonist had had his usual generous libations in the bank house.

'Where will he be going?' Archie asked his companion.

'God knows. They're a very queer family.'

'But he's harmless, isn't he?'

'There was a brother, but he died,' Gille Ruadh divulged.

'I haven't heard about him,' the banker said. 'When was this?'

'Well, Lachlan must be thirty five, so it would be about twenty years ago, before you came to the island.'

'His mother has never mentioned him in all the years that she's been coming into the bank,' Archie observed.

'That's because it was so tragic,' Gille Ruadh said.

He always told a story in his own time and slowed down his pace on the steep brae for the narrative.

'He was accused of molesting a girl.'

'Who was that, John?'

'A girl called Annie Maitland, who lived up in the council houses. She was ages with him and he used to sit on the wall, waiting for her to come out of school, though of course he didn't go himself because he wasn't right. His mother tried to teach him at home, the poor soul, but I'm afraid it was hopeless.

'Anyway, he developed this crush on Annie, I suppose you would call it. When she came out of the school he would be waiting for her and he walked her up the road, carrying her schoolbag. She wasn't a good-looking girl and I suppose she was flattered by the attention, because Tearlach had the fine features of his mother, who was considered a beauty in her day.

'This went on for weeks, if not months. Then one afternoon she didn't arrive home from school. Her mother went to some of the girl's friends and discovered that Tearlach had been walking her home. She sent for the father, who worked for the County on the roads. He was a big brute of a man from the mainland and I never liked him. He went to the sergeant and a big search was started, because the father said that Tearlach was a dangerous imbecile who had murdered his daughter.'

Gille Ruadh described the sweep of the town in his vivid Gaelic, with at least forty people out with torches and collie dogs.

'They weren't found till it was dark.'

'Was she dead, John?' the banker asked, in agonising suspense.

'As a matter of fact she wasn't. They had fallen asleep together in the hay in Jimmy MacFarlane's shed. When Annie's father arrived it took four men to hold him back from attacking Tearlach. He was shouting at the boy that he was a rapist and he would see that his doings were cut off and that he was put away in an asylum for the rest of his life where he couldn't molest girls.'

They had reached the top of the brae, where Gille Ruadh parked himself on the wall and lit a cigarette before continuing the tale.

'Dr Murdoch was called for and he examined her to see if she had been interfered with. Evidently she had, so the sergeant took Tearlach up to the police station, to keep him overnight before taking him to the mainland on the steamer.'

But the boy had run away and the next morning was found hanging from a tree on the path leading round the bay to the Ainsworthy mansion.

'One of Annie's friends came on the phone that night and asked to be put through to another girl. I happened to overhear her saying that it was Annie who had led Tearlach on.'

'So he was harmless, John?'

'That's what they say about Lachlan, but what's he doing wandering about at this time of night? If he gets into trouble and is sent to an asylum on the mainland it will kill his mother.'

But Lachlan continued to go down his grandfather's splendid silent staircase every night, his boots in his hand, with his mother sleeping easily because she believed that he was safe in his bed. He was spending all day in the loft, the hammering giving her a sore head, but at least he was occupied and not under her feet, looking for odd jobs to do in the house, because he was a thoughtful son who showed her a lot of affection.

Early one morning she came down to find the kettle almost boiled dry on the stove, but when she went up to his bedroom he wasn't there. She called to him and received a muffled answer from the loft.

'What are you doing up there at this hour?' she demanded.

'I couldn't sleep, so I thought I was as well working.'

She was looking at the ladder, wondering if she shouldn't climb up to see what he was doing up there, but she had never had a head for heights.

A fortnight later she was wakened by a hammering on the door, and when she went down in her dressing-gown the sergeant was standing on the step with her son.

'What's he done?' she asked fearfully.

That's when his activities came out, and the town was agog. The year before, MacDiarmid the boatbuilder had died and since he didn't have a son or an apprentice, the workshop was padlocked. However, one night a fishing boat, coming in late to the harbour, had seen the glimmer of a light in the workshop. Though one of the crew suggested that the ghost of the boatbuilder must have returned to the trade that he had loved and excelled in, the skipper reported the light to the police from the phone box on the seafront.

When the sergeant went down to the workshop he found that the padlock had been forced and there were signs that someone were squatting there. The sergeant suspected tinkers and waited until dawn, but no one appeared. However, he came down the following night with a flask of coffee and a blanket and Lachlan appeared around one a.m.

MacDiarmid's widow was then brought down in the patrol car and confirmed that a considerable stock of timber was missing.

'We think your son stole the wood,' the sergeant told Mrs MacDougall as he stood with Lachlan on her doorstep in the dawn. 'Where has he hidden it?'

'There's a shed at the back.'

The sergeant took Tearlach with him, but came back to report that the shed was empty.

'I don't know where else. . .' she said, then stopped.

'I think I should come in,' the sergeant said.

He went up the ladder into the loft, and when he didn't reappear Mrs MacDougall called up anxiously.

'My God,' she heard him repeat.

'What is it?' she cried in alarm from the landing. 'What has he gone and done? Please don't take him away. I've lost one already.'

That perfectly made staircase became the most used in the town that day and stout men hauled themselves up on the ladder, their head and shoulders in the loft opening. The boat rested on the rafters that Lachlan had floored. It was twelve feet long, of beautifully curved timbers gleaming with varnish, with a tiller and a mast to go into the slot on the seat. There was even a name-plate, *Tearlach*. He had cut the timbers in MacDiarmid's shed before shouldering them up the brae in the darkness, then used the boiling kettle on the stove to bend them in the steam before he had carried them up into the loft. Visitors to the loft who knew boats agreed that MacDiarmid the master craftsman would not have made a better job – especially given the restrictions.

But where had the plan for this sailing boat come from? How could a person who had hardly been to school and who was illiterate have created such perfection? When asked, Lachlan shrugged, as if he didn't understand the question. They concluded that he must have been paying far more attention to MacDiarmid while he was working with him than had been assumed at the time. But why build it in the loft instead of down in the workshop? Wasn't this another example of the insanity that was in the family?

'Are you going to charge him?' the distraught mother asked the sergeant.

'Well, he did break into the shed and steal the timber, Mrs MacDougall. It depends on Mrs MacDiarmid.'

The boatbuilder's widow said that she would let the matter go, provided that she was paid for the wood and the burst padlock. She wanted thirty pounds, which Mrs MacDougall didn't have and couldn't have repaid through a bank loan, even if she hadn't been too independent to ask Archie Maclean.

The news of the boat in the loft was conveyed to Carmichael across his beer taps in the Arms that night.

'What a shame it'll have to be broken up,' someone observed. 'They say it's a beauty. All it needs is a sail and it could go into the bay tomorrow.'

Carmichael called his wife down to attend to the bar while he drove up the brae. He had a big flashlight with him as he went up the ladder and into the loft. It was a long time before his considerable rump reappeared, but when he reached the landing he said to Lachlan: 'I'll give you three hundred pounds for it'; then, interpreting his silence as a refusal: 'all right, three fifty.'

'But you can't get it down,' the boatbuilder pointed out.

The next day Carmichael arrived with Donnelly the roofer. Within two hours he had the slates stripped, the sarking off, and then the crane that the Forestry used came up the brae and lifted out the boat, which was then conveyed on a lorry down to the bay.

Tearlach is much admired as Carmichael sails it on a summer afternoon, sitting out on the gunwale, the perfect prow cleaving the waters of the bay, the sail taut on the dead straight mast. As for Lachlan, having bought his mother a watch with the bounty from the sale of the boat, he purchased a television set for himself and now sits in front of it, watching Westerns.

18
Unnatural Activities

It was Gille Ruadh's habit to remain in the bank house until one a.m., by which time half the bottle of whisky had been consumed, and his hostess was nodding to sleep. The banker liked to walk his informant up the brae, because it gave him fresh air after a day spent in his office, and also because on the way the small man in the gangster's pearl-grey hat raised his stick to point out houses of interest, recalling characters who had lived in them.

Archie Maclean heard the story of a man called *Bodach na h-Aiseil* who lived in squalor, using a carpet as a blanket, and eating Kitty-Kat from a tin because it was cheaper – and tastier, he claimed – than the meat from the butcher's.

'Why was he called the old man of the ass, John?' his intrigued companion asked.

'Well, the family were too poor to own an ass, that's for certain. He got the name because his ears stuck out like his father's and his father before him.'

The stick swung up to a blacked-out window, where Minnie

MacLennan had lived. In Gille Ruadh's prim parlance she had been 'bad for men,' and had once entertained the entire crew of a submarine during the war. The banker knew that some of these stories had been exaggerated, but he loved them nonetheless and would himself embellish them in relating them to his customers.

One balmy post-midnight as they were going up the brae Gille Ruadh stopped. The banker thought that he wanted to relieve himself against a wall after his intake of whisky, but the stick was swinging up to a cottage.

'When I was a boy no one would go near that place.'

Except that one day, Gille Ruadh, then a message boy in the Island Emporium, with a full head of red hair, was asked to deliver a pair of trousers. He knew that it was more than his job was worth to refuse.

Fifty years later, he told the banker how he had approached the house with the parcel under his arm, his hand trembling so much that he could hardly lift the brass locker. The door had been opened by a youth, but as the message boy was handing over the item he heard a terrible crash in the house, as if all the ceilings had come down simultaneously.

'What did you do, John?' the banker asked.

'I took to my heels of course.'

When Kenneth Murdoch was studying to be a licentiate in medicine in Aberdeen he came across a shelf of books called the Proceedings of the Society for Psychical Research. Murdoch had misread the title, thinking it was physical and therefore connected to his studies in anatomy, which he found difficult. He took one of the volumes to a table in the library and began to read it. The accounts contradicted almost everything he had so far learned in medicine. The book was categorical – man had a soul. Not only that, his mind was distinct from his brain and his mind survived death as part of his soul.

Whenever he had spare time, Murdoch came into the library to take a volume of the Proceedings from the shelf. In the course of the weeks and months he read about apparitions, poltergeists, and mediums who could materialise people. Kenneth Murdoch found that he used his scalpel with much more confidence in the anatomy room because he had learned that something had survived the cadaver he had been assigned to work on.

He became a spiritualist, watching mediums demonstrating their ability to take messages from the dead and after a year, he was invited to sit in a circle in which he saw ectoplasm pouring out of a medium's mouth. He also took a deep interest in fairies, reading that they were small beings who lived under mounds on lonely moors. That was why, when he was qualified, he decided to take a post in the Hebrides. His reading had informed him that these islands contained people who had second sight and who could foretell events. He could combine observations of these phenomena with his medical duties and perhaps contribute papers to the Proceedings of the Society for Psychical Research.

Most summer evenings after surgery the doctor drove down the island in his little Austin to look for fairies on the moors. He was observed lying on his side, an ear to one of the mounds, as if trying to eavesdrop on a conversation of the little people. It was remarked that if only he applied the same concentration to listening to people's chests through his stethoscope, there wouldn't be so many sick people on the island and so many of his patients up in the cemetery.

One afternoon Dr Murdoch was called out to see a patient who was too ill to come to his surgery. The house on the brae had been built by Phemie MacAuslan's father, a sea Captain. When she was seventeen Phemie became pregnant and it was said that the father had been a tinker who had come to the house one day, offering to repair a hole in a kettle. Dr Murdoch had delivered the baby while its staunch Free Church grandparents sat grim-faced by the fire, having told their daughter that she would surely go to hell for her carnality.

But the old couple were both dead and Phemie lived in the house with her son. She took the doctor up the narrow stairs to the small bedroom with a window overlooking the bay. Though it was summer a fire was burning in the grate of blue tiles that the Captain had brought back from Holland. The boy was lying in the bed by the fire when the doctor entered, having to stoop for the low lintel.

'Well, how are you today, Alasdair?' he asked, setting his medical bag on the table by the bed where the concerned mother had been tempting her son with fruit.

The boy answered with a burst of coughing as the doctor fitted the stethoscope into his ears and listened to the querulous chest. It was a clear case of TB, the scourge of the island.

'It's a bit better today,' the doctor lied, replacing the stethoscope in his bag. 'Well, Alasdair, maybe we can get you to school in September.'

Because of his ailment the boy had barely attended. He turned his head and looked at the doctor with his large luminous eyes, a feature Murdoch had observed in many TB patients.

The mother followed the doctor out and he thought she was going to ask him about the true state of her son's health. He was preparing a vague answer, because he knew how devoted she was to her boy.

'I don't think I can go on, doctor.'

Was she telling him she suspected that she had caught the disease from her son?

'We'll go back in and I'll examine you, Phemie, but you seem healthy to me, with good colour on your cheeks.'

'It's not me, doctor, it's the things he does.'

'I don't understand, Phemie. I thought the boy was in bed for most of the time, he's got so little strength.'

'He is, but he can do things from the bed.'

'I'm lost, Phemie,' Dr Murdoch admitted.

'He lies there looking at something, then it takes off.'

'Takes off?' He was beginning to suspect that the strain of looking after her sick son was affecting her mind.

'He lies staring at the poker, then it rises from the hearth and starts to work at the fire.'

Dr Murdoch had read of such cases in the psychical books he had been absorbing since his student days.

'Let's see if anything happens,' he said as he went back inside, saying in a loud voice as he went up the stairs again: 'Thank you, Phemie, I will take a cup of tea.'

The tea came in china the Captain had brought back from a voyage to the South Seas.

'I'm very interested in the mounds on the moor down the island, Phemie,' the doctor told her. 'I believe they're occupied by fairies. Have you ever seen a fairy?'

'No, never, doctor.'

The youth was watching the doctor.

'But you believe in them?' he asked Phemie.

'Oh yes, there are more things in this world that we know about. My father had the second sight.'

'Really?' the doctor said. 'What kind of things did the Captain see?'

'Well, one day when he was walking on the moor with my mother before he went to sea the veins at his temple began to throb, as if they were going to burst. Then he said to my mother, "My uncle Dan's just been drowned at the whaling in Newfoundland. His boat overturned." He went home and lay in his bed for two days until the telegram came, confirming what he had seen in his vision.'

The occupant of the bed was listening intently, his eyes on his mother.

'I believe that,' Dr Murdoch said. 'I'm sure that some people have special powers. What do you think, Alasdair?'

The boy lay staring at him, taking it all in.

'I've read of people who can move things with their minds,'

the doctor continued. 'That must be a wonderful thing to see.'

The sick boy had turned his head on the pillow and was staring at the fire. Dr Murdoch watched the poker, but it didn't move.

'I think I'll give you something for your nerves, Phemie,' he said as she saw him out.

A yachtsman surveying the town through his binoculars from the sunny deck of his boat saw this pale face at a window half-way up the brae and thought he was seeing a ghost in sunlight.

Alasdair was declining, but there were no further visits from Dr Murdoch, because after surgery he drove down the country to eavesdrop on the fairy mounds. He had been told by one of his oldest patients that a man from the Ross 'many years before' had been wandering the moors, the worse for drink, when he was forced to lie down. His ear was next to a mound and he heard the sounds of an underground ceilidh. Clawing away the earth, he saw a tiny man playing a fiddle while naked ladies danced in a circle. The chamber was filled with smoke from miniature pipes, and there was a barrel of whisky the size of a thimble. The enraged party chased the man across the moor.

One evening after the doctor had returned from his excursion and was reading the latest volume of the Proceedings of the Society for Psychical Research to which he subscribed he heard a hammering on his door. It was Mrs MacAuslan, a shawl over her head, distraught.

'Come quickly, doctor! Something terrible's happening in the house.'

Murdoch grabbed his medical bag and drove her down the road, parking at the top of the brae. When he followed her in he was greeted by an unbelievable sight. The elephant tusk which the Captain had brought back from a voyage and which had hung on hooks over the sitting-room fire was moving around the room on its own volition, with a thrusting motion, as if the beast that it had belonged to was behind it, massive, invisible.

Now the tusk had turned and was bearing down on Murdoch.

He hardly had time to step aside before it thudded, embedding itself in the door.

'Do something!' Mrs MacAuslan was screaming.

Murdoch looked up and saw her son standing at the top of the stairs in his pyjamas.

'Did you do that to the tusk, Alasdair?' he asked.

As the boy shook his head a book came flying out of the case by the fire and struck Murdoch on the face, sending him reeling. Now all the volumes from the shelves were in motion round the room, their pages fluttering like the wings of disturbed birds.

The doctor tried to shut the door behind him, but it felt as if something with superior strength was on the other side, preventing him. He pushed Mrs MacAuslan up the stairs and into the boy's room.

Alasdair was now back in bed, lying with a hand under his chin, staring dreamily out of the window at the big moon above the bay, as if wishing himself away to a galaxy where there was no TB. Below, it sounded as if the room was being systematically destroyed.

Murdoch took the mother into a corner of the room and whispered to her: 'It may not be your boy.'

'What do you mean?'

'It could have been something your father brought back from his travels. Who knows where he got these things? That mask on the wall downstairs looks very sinister, as if it could have been used in rituals.'

'But these things have been in this house for all those years,' she pointed out. 'Why only now?'

The boy had turned his face away from the moon and was staring at the doctor, who went and sat on the edge of the bed. First he took his pulse, and then withdrew the thermometer from under his tongue, but both were normal.

'Alasdair,' he asked gently, 'why are these things happening below?'

'It's not me,' he said. 'It's the person inside me.'

stories from an island   205

'The person inside you?' his mother wailed.

'Wait a moment, Phemie,' Murdoch cautioned gently.

'What do you mean, the person inside you?'

Before the boy could answer the poker rose from the hearth and clashed between the bars, showering sparks, then clattered back, rolling across the boards and under the bed.

'Did you do that, Alasdair?' the doctor asked.

This time the mahogany plaque decorated with ivory birds which the Captain had brought back from another of his voyages fell from above the fireplace, shattering the glass ornaments on the mantelpiece.

'What are we going to do, doctor?' Mrs MacAuslan wailed, at the end of her tether.

But the doctor didn't know. This was not a medical problem, to be looked up in his textbooks. For years he had been reading about poltergeist cases in his extensive library, with, in fact, more books on the paranormal than on medicine. He had read that poltergeist activity was often associated with pre-pubescent children who denied vehemently that they were the cause of the phenomena, often violent and terrifying.

'Have you anywhere else to go?' Dr Murdoch asked the hysterical woman.

But who was going to take in a boy with TB?

It was the following day that Gille Ruadh delivered the pair of trousers on approval from the Island Emporium, and when the door was opened by the ailing boy, the messenger heard what he took to be the crashing of many ceilings. He threw the parcel in the door and ran.

'So what happened after that?' the intrigued banker asked as he and his friend ascended the brae, past the notorious house.

'It went on for another month. Dr Murdoch phoned someone high up in the Society for Psychical Research in London because my mother put through the trunk call. I believe he wanted someone to come up from London.'

A distinguished looking man with a leather portmanteau had come off the steamer and checked in at the Arms, where he and the doctor had dinner before they proceeded to the disturbed house. Dodging the flying books and ornaments, the visitor wrote up his observations in neat writing in a notebook and even when the house was filled with a roar, as if the sea had risen up from the bay and engulfed the property, he continued to write with his steady Waterman, as if he had been in similar situations before. However, by the time he went back down to the Arms he had a black eye from a ceremonial slipper which the Captain had brought back from Rangoon and which had shot up from a shelf with incredible velocity.

Two weeks later Alasdair MacAuslan died, aged twelve, and the doctor wrote 'tuberculosis' on the certificate. That night his mother lay in a peaceful house for the first time in months, though she couldn't sleep for her grief. At two a.m. as one of the Captain's clocks was striking, she was sure she felt a light kiss on her cheek.

A year later the case of the island poltergeist was published in the Proceedings of the Society for Psychical Research, because these things take time to write up. Dr Murdoch was mentioned several times and after he had read the account, he put the volume in its correct place on the shelf and began to plan his own report on fairies.

19
Aground

Every time Marsaili hears a window rattle in her Glasgow home she thinks of her mother. Come autumn Alice would put a hand to her throat and moan: 'It's going to be a bad night.' She was terrified of storms, but her husband would reassure her: 'there's not a better built house on the island, Alice. Even if there's a force 12 tonight it won't make any difference to us.'

'Oh yes it will because the electricity could go,' she persisted.

The town was lit by a generator behind the distillery, and there were power cuts when the raging burn spilled into the shed.

'Then we'll put torches and candles on the hall table,' Archie tells his nervous spouse.

'Promise me that when you retire we'll move to the mainland,' Alice pleads.

'And have nobody to speak Gaelic with?' her husband says sadly. 'Ask anything of me but that, Alice. I'm going to pour you a whisky and you're going to sit by the fire and calm yourself.'

'Oh that wind,' Marsaili can hear her mother moaning. 'My poor head.'

Marsaili did her homework at the dining-room table, with a big fire burning in the grate. She liked to hear the sea below the window as she studied. This November night she was learning Gaelic vocabulary when she heard a siren. She went to the window and saw through its rain-streaked pane the blurred lights of a big boat sliding into view, then heard the rumble of an anchor.

'Was that thunder?' her father asked, coming through to stand at the window beside her. 'No, it's the boat for the Outer Isles. It must have had to come in for shelter. Don't tell your mother, or she'll be thinking there's going to be a hurricane.'

Half an hour later the doorbell rang. Marsaili went down, forcing open the storm door against the wind. A dark figure was standing in a long coat streaming with rain. The light was on above his head and a badge in the shape of a gold anchor gleamed on his peaked cap.

'Is your father in?' he asked in Gaelic in a rich island voice.

Ten minutes later Archie came into the dining-room with the visitor.

'This is my daughter Marsaili. She's doing her Gaelic home-work.'

'Very good,' the visitor said, nodding.

'Put your books away because you're going to get a lesson in Gaelic,' her father told her. 'Captain Kennedy is one of the great tradition-bearers of the Hebrides. We're lucky the storm sent his boat in. If you hear a word you don't understand, interrupt us.'

The banker poured the Captain a large whisky from the trolley and as they settled at the fire, Marsaili turned her chair.

'What kind of story would you like?' the Captain asked her with a smile.

'Marsaili is deeply into the supernatural, and you come from an island with many stories,' her father said.

'It's certainly the night for such a story,' the Captain conceded. 'But maybe Marsaili won't sleep if I tell her what happened to me.'

'I will,' she said resolutely.

This was going to be a leisurely story because there was obviously no prospect of the boat sailing that night. The Captain took a sip of his whisky, lit a cigarette, and explained that he came from an island twenty miles to the west. He had been raised on a croft and had left school at fifteen. He had wanted to go deep sea like his uncles but his mother, who was a widow, needed him to help with the croft, so he became an assistant steward on the steamer. As he describes the summer cruises the wind at Marsaili's back seems to abate and the room is full of light and warmth. She can see the sparkling silver cutlery with the crossed pennants of the steamer company being laid on the starched white cloth beside the little white tent of the linen napkin. Couples come down for lunch, the women in cloche hats, the men with two-tone shoes, to sit at the open portholes, holding hands and sometimes leaning over to kiss. Up on the deck, McNally the resident musician, sober so far, entertains the trippers to a selection of Hebridean airs on his hammer dulcimer beside the big red funnel. The Captain's Gaelic is so melodious that Marsaili can hear the tinkle of *The Road to the Isles* in it.

'I got tired of serving steak pie and dishes of potatoes,' the Captain confessed, 'so I went to the nautical college in Glasgow to better myself.'

He studied hard for his certificates and became a mate at the age of twenty two. He was on the bridge one stormy night when the Captain took a heart attack.

'We did our best for him but he was dead within ten minutes, so there I was, left to look after the wheel.'

His Gaelic became even more eloquent as he relived the experience of that night: the seas mounting over the sides, swamping the vehicles lashed to the deck. However, he had brought the boat safely into the pier, without any damage to either. 'I would have been a Captain before I was thirty but the war came and I joined the navy.'

He went down south for training, but in the autumn of 1940

his mother had become seriously ill and he went home to the island on compassionate leave.

'She was expected to go at any moment and to tell you the truth, I wanted to see the poor soul at rest because of the pain she was in,' her son said as the wind shook the dining-room window, blurring the lights of his boat. He took another sip of whisky. 'One night – it must have been about two in the morning – I heard her calling out and I went through to her room. What is it, mother? "I was dreaming," she said. "I saw you among the dead." Well I don't mind telling you I got a bad fright because she had the second sight. But I had to calm her down so I said: "there's nothing going to happen to me, mother. It's only a bad dream you've been having." She died at five that morning.'

When he said this, his Gaelic began to falter, and his host refilled his whisky glass.

'They allowed me another week of leave for the funeral and to sort out her effects. Not that there was much to sort out. She wasn't a woman of worldly possessions but she was full of Gaelic songs and stories and the house was empty without her.'

The grieving son went for a long walk along the strand on the western side of the island on a beautiful autumn evening, with the sun sinking into the sea.

'I was thinking about my future. If I survived the war, would I want to come back to the island, now that both my parents were dead? I was also thinking about death,' the Captain confessed, sipping more of his dram. 'I was asking myself as I walked along the strand: would I see my parents again in the next life? Having seen a boat torpedoed and all the poor souls drowned, I had lost my faith. The stories I had heard at our fireside on windy nights about the second sight I no longer believed in.

'So there I was, on the strand that evening, so beautiful and calm that you wouldn't believe a war was going on. That's when I became aware that I was walking among five seamen. I saw there was something strange about them. I couldn't see the prints of their seaboots on the wet sand. Though the hoods of their duffel coats were up, I could see their faces against the sky, and there was something terribly wrong with them. I was very frightened, I tell you, and when I got home I said a special Gaelic prayer we have on our island if we see something that's not of this world.'

He repeated the prayer, with the window at his back shaking.

'I thought: I'm not staying another night on this island. I'll get the boat in the morning and have a couple of days in Glasgow. I packed my case and thought about locking up the house, because I knew that I wouldn't see it for a long time. In fact I didn't care if I never saw it again. I had lost my mother, and had had that frightening experience with the five men who vanished in front of my eyes on the shore.'

'Not even the old men on the island had seen anything like the mist that rolled in from the sea overnight, so thick that you couldn't see your hand in front of you,' the Captain said. 'The steamer couldn't come from the mainland and the island was cut off.

'I couldn't step over the threshold of the house because of the mist. I had a crystal wireless, but it didn't work well and I had no newspapers, so I was bored. I was also angry at not getting away, because I really didn't want to spend another night on the island. Next morning there was a knock on my door.'

He paused to sip his whisky.

'Do you want to hear the rest of this story, Marsaili?'

'Yes please,' she pleaded.

'It's not a pleasant story,' he warned.

'You may as well tell her, Iain,' the banker said. 'One thing's for certain: she's getting the best lesson in Gaelic she's ever had in her life.'

The local coastguard was standing on Captain Kennedy's step, telling him that his services were needed because a boat had run aground on the Stirks, the notorious reef off the west coast of the island.

'The mist was still thick. I climbed on to the lorry and we drove across the island. We stood on the shore but we couldn't see a thing. We took the boat out very slowly towards the reef because there was a heavy sea running. Suddenly we saw this grey shape ahead. It was a big boat and it was lying at an angle on the Stirks about half a mile away. My God, I thought, it's the steamer, the one I used to sail in. We couldn't approach any closer because it was too dangerous.'

The way the Captain was telling the story, Marsaili could see the grey ship looming ahead.

But it wasn't the steamer whose dining saloon he had served in. A destroyer had got lost in the fog and had been frightened to use its wireless for help in case the message was picked up by a U-boat. The boat's back had broken on the reef and it was taking in water.

'We were making our way out to it when a boat bumped into us, almost capsizing us. It was a ship's lifeboat, upside down. We searched around and saw bodies. They were wearing duffel coats and seaboots and when we lifted them out of the water their faces were all swollen up because of the salt. That's when I understood what my mother had meant about being among the dead. These five bodies were the men I had been walking among on the shore two nights before.'

Marsaili is so chilled by the climax to the story that she can't move. She hears the Captain explaining to her father that the five men had panicked when the destroyer ran aground and took to one of the lifeboats. They were the only casualties among a thousand men.

'The fog lifted that afternoon,' the Captain went on, 'and another destroyer took the men off. Then the wind got up and overnight the boat was a wreck. We buried the five bodies on the island and men came later from the War Graves Commission and put up stones. When I'm home I always go to put flowers from the garden on the five graves.'

Alice comes in with tea and sandwiches at that point and starts quizzing the Captain, asking him if the weather is going to get worse. Marsaili wants to push her mother out of the room so that their visitor can tell other stories, but Alice has sat down and is reminiscing with him about big winds.

The Captain went away at ten, kissing Marsaili on the cheek and telling her to work hard at her Gaelic lessons. But she couldn't concentrate on her vocabulary book after he had gone into the stormy night. She turned her chair to the window and watched the big lighted boat through the rain–streaked glass. Their visitor had left her with a new word – *taibhse*, a ghost. She kept the light on that night and by next morning the steamer had gone, as if it had come in a dream, and Alice was calm again.

20
Ecstasy

Every night when she should have been doing her homework – 'if you are to make anything of your life,' her mother said – Jo was sitting at her computer, either e-mailing friends she had seen that day, or else surfing the Web. She downloaded music to listen to, and joined a fan-club chat-room for her favourite band The Dark Princes. The fifteen year old's ambition was to get a well-paid job on the mainland so that she could afford to go to the gigs of her leather-clad heroes. She had a t-shirt of the band pinned to the wall above her bed and touched it before she slept every night.

Jo practically lived on the Web. The cosmetics on the tray on her dressing-table had been bought on the Web, using her mother's Visa card, and most of the clothes in her wardrobe had been purchased on eBay, where she made successful bids for zany second-hand outfits.

'You spend too much time on that computer,' her father complained. He belonged to the generation who had sat round temperamental television sets, watching soaps and sports programmes in black and white. Before the war, his mother told him, people in the town sat round their living flame fires and conversed in Gaelic, sometimes telling stories about the supernatural until it felt as if there were a ghost in the room.

But Jo wasn't interested in her grandmother's stories about the supernatural. She was deeply into The Dark Princes, who claimed descent from the Goths.

One night a pop-up in the corner of her computer screen advises Jo that she has a message.

'Hi, my name is David, and I live in Glasgow and am a dedicated fan of The Dark Princes. I saw what you wrote in the chat-room, and I'm making contact.'

Jo replied that it was 'good to hear from another fan of this cool band. What's your favourite record by them?'

In the following weeks they exchanged experiences. David told her how he had attended a concert of the band's in Glasgow, 'and everyone was jumping about with excitement – and other things.'

'What do you mean – other things?' Jo typed back.

'I mean a pill called Ecstasy. Hasn't it reached your island yet? It's wonderful for giving you a lift, and when you take it before the band starts up you feel that they're playing within your head.'

'It sounds fantastic. I would like to try Ecstasy,' she replied.

The first drug to arrive on the island (apart from tobacco in the sixteenth century) was a reefer in the pocket of a university drop-out who came to the island in the early 1970s. His hair was down to his shoulders and he slept in a tent on a croft at the top of the town. One night when he was among a crowd listening to the Doors on the jukebox in the Sea Breezes Café he rolled a slim cigarette and proceeded to light up.

'What kind is that?' one of the girls asked.

'It's a magic one.'

'Magic?' she queried.

'You won't buy this in a tobacconist's,' he told her. 'It s called cannabis.'

'Never heard of it,' the girl, who was addicted to Embassy cigarettes, replied.

'Try it,' the student offered, holding it out.

The girl took a draw of the slim cigarette, and soon felt its effect ascending into her head, giving her a feeling she had never experienced before, not even from drinking double vodkas in the Arms before a dance.

'What is it?' she enquired.

'It's a drug the hippies in California use to tune them into music,' he told her, taking back the illicit smoke. 'If you like I can get you some.'

'How much does it cost?' she asked.

'It's more expensive than ordinary cigarettes, but then, it isn't an ordinary smoke.'

The next week he passed her a little sack of marijuana, to roll into her own cigarettes, and she handed over ten pounds. She smoked one each evening, lying on her bed, and felt that she was floating out over the bay. At school she shared one with her friends, and they bought some from the university drop-out.

Then harder drugs like heroin arrived, and one boy actually injected himself until his arms looked as if they had been attacked by blood-sucking insects. He had to go to the mainland for his supplies. Heroin was much more expensive than cannabis, and he started to steal to finance his addiction. When he was stopped at the door of a store in the mainland port with an expensive leather jacket in a carrier bag, the police were called, and the sheriff sent him for rehabilitation treatment.

'Send me an Ecstasy tablet,' Jo repeated in her e-mail.

'It's too dangerous,' David mailed back. 'You need to come down here to try it, under supervision.'

'Do you mean come to Glasgow?' Jo typed.

'Yes. Why don't you come on the 28th of next month, when the band is playing? I can get us tickets because I know one of the roadies.'

Jo told her mother that she was going to the concert on the mainland with two of her friends.

'I don't like the idea,' Betty said anxiously. 'You're only fifteen.'

'I've had my period for three years,' her daughter answered. 'Some girls of my age are married and have children.'

'Who told you this?' her mother wanted to know.

'I read it on the Web. I've even seen pictures of the babies.'

'You're too much on that computer,' Betty complained. 'We'll have to wait and see what your father says about this trip to Glasgow.'

But Jo knew that she could get round her father and, once he heard that two of her friends were going, he gave his consent – and fifty pounds.

Jo was wearing denims and a zipped jacket lined with fleece when her mother saw her on to the bus, slipping her a twenty pound note with instructions to 'look after yourself and watch crossing the street.' Once on the ferry Jo took her case into the toilet and changed into a long black dress and boots that laced up to her knees, a Goth outfit she had bought on eBay but which her parents had never seen.

She took the train to Glasgow and then a taxi to the flat where she was to meet David. It was in the west end of the city and she noticed the garbage in the street and the boarded-up windows. She climbed the worn stairs and rang the bell on the second floor landing as she had been instructed.

'Is David in?' she asked the person who answered the door.

'I'm David.'

Jo was taken aback, but then saw her mistake. Father and son shared the same name.

'David your son, I mean.'

'I don't have a son. You're Jo, aren't you?'

Perhaps she would not have stepped over this threshold if she hadn't noticed the poster on the wall at the end of the lobby. It was of The Dark Princes, and she had been outbid for it on eBay, because it was now a collector's item, with the band's international fame.

Jo had a moment of panic when she heard the chain being put on the door behind her.

'You can't be too careful, with the kind of people we get about here,' David explained. 'Come on in.'

When she follows him into the lounge she has the opportunity to have a good look at her host, though the blinds are down. He must be in his thirties, possibly older, she estimates. She is surprised that someone of his age is a fan of The Dark Princes. He is entirely in black, from his pointed shoes to his spiky hair that looks greased. A chain is looped from his left earlobe to the corner of his mouth, and there is a poster of the group on the wall, as well as one of the band's CDs playing on the hi-fi.

'How long have you followed the Princes?' she asks as he sits beside her on the sofa, wondering if she has made a mistake, coming here.

'Since the first day I heard them in Glasgow. It was at the back of a pub, and I knew then that they would make it big because their sound was so funky.'

'And did they wear the same gear?' she asks.

'Some of the same gear. They had the boots up to their knees. But the studded jackets and the metalwork through their nose and lips came later. I'll show you something.'

He goes to a drawer and brings back a photograph which has been sealed in plastic. It's of the band, and it's signed: 'to David, one of our first fans'.

'That must be worth a lot,' Jo says enviously.

'I suppose I could get two grand for it on eBay, but I'm not selling.'

Where is the Ecstasy tablet he wrote about in the chat-room?

That's the question Jo wants to put to him, but he's gone through to the kitchen to cook her something while she sits listening to the CD of her adored band, the signed photograph on the lap of her black dress. David returns with two plates of Thai curry which he made himself, not from a packet. It's hot and she has to ask for a glass of water. After he's washed up the dishes it's time to go to the concert.

There are hundreds standing in the auditorium, but David's two tickets are for the tiered seats, towards the front rows. When the band comes leaping on stage Jo is on her feet, yelling with two thousand other fans who have paid big money for this privilege. The energy of the band sweeps in waves through the vast auditorium, up to the tiers where Jo and David are sitting. Jo is dazzled by the flash of guitar strings, the strobe of the lights, the way the lead singer seems to be chewing the mike. She is on her feet until the person behind tugs her black dress.

Jo would love to have an autograph, but the queue is so long and besides, David promises he'll get one for her, because these are his friends.

'Where are you staying?' David asks, and Jo names the small hotel her parents use when they are in the city and where her mother has reserved a room for her, with a private shower.

'Let's go back to my place and listen to some records,' David suggests.

He has concealed blue lights in the lounge which sweep across the posters as the CD plays, as if the band with its deafening acoustics is playing in the room.

'What about the Ecstasy tablet?' Jo shouts across to her host, whom she trusts perfectly now, after her initial apprehension. He has been so kind to her, and is going to get her an autographed photograph of her heroes.

He goes to the kitchen and brings back a jug of water and two glasses and two tablets.

Jo has not made contact, and Betty is getting more and more anxious.

'I phoned the hotel but she's not back.'

'The concert may still be going on,' her husband suggests.

'At midnight? I think you should phone the parents of her friends who went with her. Surely they've heard from them.'

Colin makes the two calls, but the girls are at home, not in Glasgow.

'She lied to us,' Betty says, more anxious than angry. 'I wish I had the number of the place where the concert's being held. Can you not find it?'

'I'll go and see if there's anything on her computer.'

He goes up the stair and stands on the threshold of his daughter's room. It's eerie, the way the moonlight is shining on the computer screen, as if it's been left on. He boots it up and finds it's not protected by a password. Colin knows that this is a violation of his daughter's privacy, but her mother is getting distraught downstairs, and he has to do something.

He opens the Inbox of her e-mails and begins scrolling through them. He notes the recipient's name David and begins to read them, his hands beginning to shake so much that he hits the wrong keys. She appears to have gone to Glasgow to take Ecstasy with this stranger. He has read in the newspapers about a young girl who died, dehydrated, at a rave in Ayrshire, after taking Ecstasy. What is he going to tell his wife downstairs?

But at least he has the name of the place where the concert was staged, and he gets the number from directory enquiries. The phone rings and rings, then a recorded voice informs him that the box office will not open again until nine a.m. tomorrow.

He sits for a long time staring at the screen, as if it's a photographic album in which he can see images of his daughter, the pictures he took of her at the sandy bay on the west coast of the island; the gawky ten year old with the brace on her teeth.

The following morning he called in the police, and a computer specialist came off the ferry that evening. Within half an hour he was in the chat-room, scrutinising the exchanges between Jo and David.

'Any leads?' Colin asked when he brought him up a mug of tea.

'It looks like a case of grooming, an older man chatting with a girl on the Web, then arranging to meet her. Whoever he is, he's been mailing your daughter from internet cafés, so that's going to make it very difficult to trace him.'

Betty has taken to her bed, under sedation, while the computer expert works upstairs. She had read cases in the newspapers about abducted girls, and sees her naked daughter, a strangled Ophelia nailed up under floorboards.

It's three months since Jo disappeared, and the computer specialist has long since gone, taking the computer's hard-drive with him. But Colin has replaced it and sits night after night in front of the screen, waiting for a message. There are many pop-ups, from eBay, and e-mails from fans of The Dark Princes, and plaintive messages in the chat-room.

'Where are you, Jo?' That's when Colin decides to post a message, asking if anyone knows of the whereabouts of his daughter.

But Jo wasn't under the floorboards in David's house. She was standing in the kitchen, a chain between earlobe and lip, preparing their Thai curry supper. On the night that she had insisted on popping the Ecstasy pill she had had a bad experience, and if it weren't for David's ministrations, she would have died. He poured jugs of water into her to stop her becoming dehydrated, and sat up with her all night until she recovered, blaming himself for having given her the pill. He didn't sexually assault her; it was she who threw herself on him the following morning because she saw how kind and loving he was towards her – and, of course, he had a signed photograph of The Dark Princes.

'Did you know I was fifteen?' she asked.

'Honestly, no, I thought I was in the chat-room with a nineteen – even a twenty year old.'

She should have phoned her parents, but she knew that they would blame David for luring her from home, and that they would call in the police. Not that she wanted to go back to the island, with its one street, and not even a CD shop. After all, in a year she would be coming down to hairdressing college in the city.

The baby conceived under Ecstasy on the night of The Dark Princes gig lies sleeping in a carry-cot in the training salon while Jo learns how to tint. When she's qualified she will take her son to the island to meet his grandparents.

Other Books
from Argyll Publishing

Tobermory Days
Lorn Macintyre
ISBN:1 902831 56 X pbk £7.99

In this first collection of stories, Lorn Macintyre captures the
range and depth of the lives of people under a fast-changing and
fast-fading West Highland cloud.
'compelling and exhilarating' **West Highland Free Press**

Selected Stories
Brian McCabe
ISBN: 1 902831 62 4 pbk £9.99

This carefully selected choice by the author shows
the sharp, stylish, moving and funny nature of this
original and inventive mind.
'a writer whose craft is polished to the point of invisibility'
The Scotsman

The Wind in her Hands
Margaret Gillies Brown
ISBN:1 902831 41 1 pbk £7.99

Gillies Brown turns her attention to the life of her own mother
whose extraordinary achievements stemmed from humble
beginnings as the daughter of a North East farm.
'an intriging picture of life early last century' **Caledonia**
'it never flags – the story of a strong woman' **Moray Firth Radio**
'inspirational' **Press & Journal**

Available in bookshops or direct from Argyll Publishing,
Glendaruel, Argyll PA22 3AE Scotland
For credit card, full stock list and other enquiries
tel 01369 820229   argyll.publishing@virgin.net
or visit our website www.argyllpublishing.com